CW00394498

The Decimation of Mae

By D H Sidebottom

Edited by: Kyra Lennon

Cover by: Ker Dukey

The Decimation of Mae

Copyright © 2014

By D H Sidebottom

For Ker Dukey.
Without you, this book simply wouldn't be.
You're my friend, my rock and my sanity.
Love you, babe <3

Table of Contents:

`

Chapter Twenty Two

'And so it ends.'

Epilogue

'And so it begins.'

The end

Prologue

The Devil visited me three times in my life; albeit, my short life. Not in the physical sense, you must understand, but very much literally.

He was persistent, resolute and tenacious. His ruthless greed to annihilate me was utterly disturbing. I am sure if he had hierarchy, the man at the top would have dragged his arse into Hell's prison for his unscrupulous methods.

I was just fifteen when I first became aware of what he was capable of. This initial taste of him set the playing field for how my life was to be *lived* – for want of a better word.

He mocked me, showed me mercilessly how he played the game and how he liked to cheat at said game. He ridiculed and taunted me until, six months later, he won and took something of so much importance from me that I would never be the same again.

His second visit was, in my eyes, so much more cruel and heartless. I know we're talking about the Devil here, and yes, you have a right to say he had no heart but even then, even when I was so utterly broken, I begged to differ and hoped – no, prayed – that somewhere deep in the caverns of his black, tortured soul there was something that beat and confused his emotions once in a while.

The third visit was somewhat different than the other two. He tried, and at first succeeded to bring me to my knees once and for all, but then something happened. God finally intervened and altered Satan's intention; he sent hope and morphed the Devil's minion into an Angel, hoping to break and shatter the anguish and suffering. He gave the ability for me to feel pleasure in pain, order in the chaos and light in the darkness.

But in giving me a reprieve, he also gave me something that would finally and ultimately obliterate me. He gave me the capability to love, therefore giving me the ability to be destroyed.

And Satan made sure that I *was* destroyed. Cruelly, viciously and sadistically.

I am Mae Swift, and this is the story of my decimation.

Chapter One

'The rule of ignorance denies our
attempt at life.'

Aged 15

"So, Mae, how are you today?"

I quirked an eyebrow at the seemingly stupid woman in front of me as she twisted the cap of her pen in her fingers and tipped her head in companion to her question. The light shone through the window, capping her bleach-blonde hair, giving her an almost angelic form.

"Oh, just super, darling."

The edge of her lips twisted slightly but other than that she showed no reaction to my reply. "How are you getting on with Mr and Mrs Braithwaite?"

I tilted my own head and looked at her with confusion. "Is that what they're called? Mr and Mrs Braithwaite?"

Her eyes narrowed, clearly misunderstanding my sarcasm. "Yes. What do you call them, Mae?"

I scoffed and blew out a small breath. "Lazy fat bastard and lily-livered bitch."

Stacey's fingers stilled, her forehead frozen with multiple creases. The pen lid flicked from her fingers and hit the bookcase across the room. She sucked in her lips, her eyes blinking rapidly as she regarded me curiously. "Is there anything I need to know about your carers?"

"Carers?" I mused the term in my head for a moment and smirked. "Yeah, that seems suitable for them. They enjoy being cared for."

Her eyes scanned my face before a pitying expression covered hers, her passionate blue eyes turning grey with sadness. "Mae, you know I can't help you unless you are completely honest with me. If the Braithwaite's aren't supervising you properly then we can arrange alternative accommodation."

I barked out a bitter laugh. "Accommodation? Wow, now I feel extra special."

She sighed and rubbed at her temples in frustration then sat back further into her chair and crossed her legs, giving me a quick flash of her plain white knickers. "Dr Fruhard tells me you had another incident last week." She leaned forward to observe me more closely; her eyes penetrating mine deeply so she could get an angle on my response as she crossed her arms across her stomach, enveloping herself protectively against my bitterness. "Can you tell me why that was?"

I shrugged. "I can but I won't."

Stacey nodded as if expecting my answer. "So, can you tell me how you feel when you cut?"

"I can but I won't," I repeated, my disturbed side relishing the quick flash of annoyance across her face.

She steepled her fingers and rested her elbows on her knees as she gave out a long-suffering sigh. "Is there anything you can tell me today, Mae?"

I studied her, taking in for the first time how pretty my psychologist really was. Her slightly curved nose was a little too small for the roundness of her face, her soft pink lips were thin but perfectly bowed and the dimple in her chin gave her a trusting appearance, if that was possible. But I didn't trust her, far from it.

I leaned towards her and smiled in surrender. Her eyes glinted as she became aware of my compliance. "I do have something to share." She nodded and gave me an encouraging smile. "I'm wearing the same knickers as you. BHS white cotton briefs, super soft and made with 50% elastane for comfort and shape."

She pursed her lips and exhaled heavily. "Yeah, they are comfy. I generally prefer thongs but they aren't appropriate for the workplace. Sometimes they can give you quite the wedgie when you're sitting all day, especially in these chairs."

I tried to hide my amusement but she caught it and winked before she stood. "We'll call it a day then, Mae."

I tilted my head then rose from my chair. I watched her walk over to her desk then place her notebook and pen on top of her anally ordered bureau. She kept her back to me but I felt her despair. There was nothing actually wrong with her but I didn't trust anyone, it was just in my make-up, the way my body was genetically built.

"He hits her," I offered simply.

Stacey turned to me, her eyes wide. "Mr Braithwaite?"

I nodded, giving her a little something just for the thong comment. "Then he leaves me to tend to her while he goes to the pub and gets off his head."

She pulled in a breath. "I'll arrange a transfer."

I nodded again but wondered where *accommodation* number three would see me.

"Thank you, Mae," she said quietly as I opened the door.

I halted and kept my palm flat on the handle as my gaze remained on the deep brown wood of the door. "It helps me release the grief," I whispered before I left the room, slowly and quietly pulling the door shut behind me.

Chapter Two

'As the Devil takes us, ghosts
strengthen us.'

Aged 18

I rolled my eyes as Liam clumsily cupped my left breast. "Come on, Mae."

The sad twat had been trying to take my virginity for over three months; he should have known I wasn't going to give in by now.

"Fuck off, Liam," I shouted in his ear over the dense thump of the music. The room was bouncing, some random guy's party filling the whole of the university campus with his choice in techno beat tunes.

I moved my head to the side and pulled in another drag before handing the joint to Liam while I held the smoke in my lungs to bring on the high that little bit quicker.

I narrowed my eyes on the tall, dark-haired guy watching me. He lifted an eyebrow at my glare but didn't shift his eyes from my face. He seemed to radiate a calm serenity that made me narrow my eyes and study him properly.

I wasn't concerned whether he considered my action rude, or even if it pissed him off, I just felt the draw of him and needed to figure out what it was about him that pulled on my senses.

Liam continued to paw me as I analysed the voyeur. His lips twisted in humour when he noticed my shameless perusal. He ran a hand through his thick brown hair, as though straightening it just for my exploration. His eyes were just as brown, rich and chocolaty but with the slightest hint of bronzed copper. The cruel smirk on his mouth paraded the fullness of his pale lips, but it was the contours of his sculptured face which made him seem almost sinful. The dusting of stubble across his chin and neck added to his rough appeal, and the prominence of his Adam's apple alerted me to his satisfaction with my attention.

I sighed as Liam's hand tried to skate under my denim skirt, his rough fingers grabbing awkwardly at my inner thigh. I punched him in the chest and scowled at him. "I said no."

His eyes transformed, his usual soft appearance morphing into one of twisted malice as he sank his fingers into the soft flesh between my legs.

"Liam!" I exclaimed as his fingers probed forbiddingly at the crotch of my knickers. "Stop it, I said!"

He pushed his body against mine and trapped me against the hallway wall, his heavy frame penning me immobile underneath him. "I'm sick of your taunts, Mae; it's about time you put out."

I scoffed at him as I tried to push him away. "No, Liam. I've never taunted you. In fact, I can't have made it more obvious that I don't wanna have sex with you."

"Stop being so fucking frigid," he snarled, prompting my anger to flare. Liam was usually quite timid and laid back. Fair enough, he had persistently tried to get into my knickers but he had never been quite so physical about it.

We'd been 'dating', if that was an appropriate word to describe our turbulent on/off relationship, for around three months. I was only with him for the coke and I'll admit he was a fairly good kisser, but he didn't appeal to me in any other way.

My eyes widened when one of his hands slid further up my skirt and the other grabbed my neck, his long, thin fingers circling my throat. "I'm not listening to no anymore, Mae. You've been mine for a while; it's about time you paid for all the snow I've been feeding your fucking nostrils."

It wouldn't be true to say I panicked but a slither of fear crawled through my veins as his eyes darkened further. I was in trouble, yet I knew it was my own fault. I'd taken from him and I knew he'd want payment for the goods soon enough.

"Liam, please. Not here."

He leaned further in, the scent of something toxic flickering across my nostrils as his rancid breath told me he'd been doing more than just coke. His fingers tightened around my neck as his teeth ground with the tension in his jaw.

I blinked as the voyeur appeared behind Liam. He locked my eyes with his as he slowly moved his mouth to Liam's ear. "The lady said no."

His voice was low and quiet. His eyes were as calm as the expression on his face yet he still seemed to be furious without any physical appearance to confirm it. He exuded raw fury and disgust but didn't exhibit it. It was hard to explain but I shivered as something disturbing crept through my bones.

"Nowt to do with you mate, piss off," Liam muttered as he flicked a glance over his shoulder.

"I think you're hurting her."

I frowned at the sudden chill in his tone as he blinked slowly. Liam didn't seem to sense it as he snorted and glanced over his shoulder. "You think?"

Voyeur smiled at me and lifted a finger as if telling me he'd be one moment. He turned around and I watched the rise and fall of his shoulders as he took a heavy inhalation, then he turned and encompassed the back of Liam's head in his large hand, gripped tight and yanked his head back.

"The lady asked you nicely. I asked you nicely. I think you should learn some fucking manners."

He then drove Liam's head into the wall in a single forceful shove. My jaw dropped as Liam fell to the floor instantly, his nose shattered and blood smeared across his face.

I lifted my eyes to Voyeur and stared in shock. He didn't seem to notice my astonishment as he smiled and extended his elbow. "May I escort you home? You look rather dazed and I'm a little worried about your safety."

I continued to gawp as I flicked glances between him and Liam. He remained silent and calm as he waited for me to decide whether he was a safer bet than taking myself home unaccompanied. "Uhh."

He chuckled lightly as his cheeks reddened with a deep flush. "Excuse me, but men who presume sort of irritate me. Nobody seems to have any manners anymore." His smile softened when he saw my wariness, and he held out his hand. "Daniel Finn. It's a pleasure to meet you..."

"Mae." I coughed to clear the lump from my throat and placed my hand in his. "Mae Swift."

His grip was strong, yet warm and courteous, and I softened slightly, my concern ebbing away. "Well, it was lovely meeting you, Mae Swift. You take care getting home."

I nodded and smiled cautiously. "Yes, you too and um, thank you."

He smiled wider, his eyes brightening; his grin eased my nerves a little. "My pleasure." He turned and strolled down the hallway.

Liam moaned beside me and I dropped my eyes to see him stirring. "Wait," I shouted after Daniel before I could change my mind. "If the offer's still there...?"

He turned and nodded. "Of course." He gave me a slow smile and held out his hand for me to take.

"Thank you." I slipped my hand in his. A small ripple of something slid through his fingers as he gently encased my fingers in his.

"Again, my pleasure."

We were silent for a few minutes as we walked. It was a cool winter's night and the chill was welcoming after the heat from the party. "Where are we heading?" Daniel asked finally as we reached the end of the street.

"The Becks estate." I grimaced slightly. Although the area was considered 'neglected' I had never been embarrassed or bothered about where I lived. The people in my block were okay and kept themselves to themselves but something about this man had me wishing for more. Maybe a part of me wanted his acceptance, or at least I didn't want his judgment.

He smiled and nodded, his face still a blank canvas. "So how long have you and your boyfriend been together?" He flicked me a glance but there was nothing on his face that showed his interest in the answer.

"We're not really together as such, more just..."

"Friends who get high?" he cut in when I couldn't find the right word to describe what Liam and I were.

My eyes widened at his bluntness. "Well..." I sighed as I squinted to consider a different description but confirmed his statement with a shrug. "I suppose."

"Mmm." He nodded slowly as his tongue pushed patterns into his cheek. "How old are you, Mae?"

"How old are you?" I retorted angrily. Fuck him and his high up judgements.

A flicker of something slithered across his face but it was gone as soon as it appeared. "Twenty five."

I was surprised, my lips pursing slightly by his answer. I had expected him to at least be slightly evasive but he seemed open and honest. "Eighteen."

He turned to look at me and smiled gently. "Well, I admire you."

"I'm sorry, I don't follow."

His hand tightened slightly as though he was praising me with a squeeze. None of his actions were what I would class as *normal*, but then who was, really? "Your refusal to give your boyfriend what he's after. It shows your strength, Mae. It tells me a lot about you."

"Oh really?" I wasn't sure if I was offended by his assessment of me or glad of his appraisal. I blinked as I tried to figure him out but it was impossible. Part of me wanted to know everything about him, and wanted him to know everything about me yet another part warned me off, alerted my senses to something that didn't fit right.

"Yes. A lot of *girls* your age lose what they are all about too early. They have no respect for themselves, but they expect others to value them. I'm afraid when that step is taken, you will never get it back and because of that you must treat it as something priceless and precious. Something irreplaceable."

"I suppose. I've always seen my virginity as something to hold on to. The last piece of me, if you get me?"

Why the hell were we talking about my virginity? I hardly knew the guy but his presence, his dominance, expected it. But why I was allowing his authority to control me and the conversation was beyond me.

"So, Mae, tell me about yourself."

"There's nothing to tell." I smiled and relaxed as the conversation veered into safer territory.

"Oh, I don't believe that. You seem full of life. You must have a few stories to tell."

"Nope."

He narrowed his eyes on me and gave me a small smirk. "Okay, I'll take a guess then. I'm an expert at reading people."

I lowered my face and smiled at my feet. He really thought he knew it all, knew me. He'd need a crystal ball to take a guess at my life.

"I think," he started, "I think you were born eighteen years ago."

I couldn't help but chuckle. "Wow, you're good."

He nodded. "See? An expert."

"That you are. What else do your super powers tell you?"

"Well, I think you're naturally black but dye your hair blonde."

"Very good." I smiled when I remembered my roots needed doing.

"You're into rock music," he offered. I gave him a nod as I glanced down at my Guns 'n Roses T-shirt.

"You're..." His eyes raked over my body. A shiver wrapped around me when he lifted his eyes back up and exposed a heat that no one had ever displayed before. My chest heaved as his tongue swept his bottom lip slowly. "Very beautiful."

I turned my face away from him to smile as a deep blush crept up my neck and flooded my cheeks. "You're also very shy," he added with a laugh.

"Not usually." I turned back to him. "But you're very forward."

He shook his head in disbelief. "I'm forward for telling you that you're beautiful?"

"Well..."

"Has anyone ever told you that you're beautiful before, Mae?"

"Will you stop! My face is on fire."

He laughed deeply, his eyes coming to life with the happy rumble. "And it makes you even more stunning," he whispered as he leant into my ear.

I blew out a slow, steady breath when his closeness seemed to ignite the fire from my face around my body. Heat rippled across every inch of my skin as his low whisper developed a need inside me that demanded attention.

"Oh," I stuttered. "This is me."

He frowned in confusion then blinked and moved back, his head turning to my apartment block when he realised I meant my home. "Already?" he whispered, his eyes raking over the building. His tone screamed disappointment and he grimaced at the sight of the weather worn paint and crumbling brickwork.

He turned back to me and took my hand into his, his thumb stroking softly across my knuckles. "I'm not sure I like you living here. It doesn't look... safe."

I laughed at him and shook my head. Once again, his forwardness amused me. "I've been here for two years, Daniel. I can guarantee I'm as safe here as anywhere else."

He shook his head and flicked another glance towards my home. "It looks like it would collapse if you sneezed."

"Then I'll make sure not to sneeze while I'm on the loo. I'd be mortified if they found me with my knickers around my ankles, still sat on the toilet."

His head snapped to the side and his eyes widened. I winked at him as I took to the entrance path. "Goodbye, Daniel. Thank you for bringing me home."

It occurred to me that he was the only man ever to have made sure I got home safe. Liam was usually passed out on the floor when I left his, and any previous date I'd had never bothered once they found out I didn't want sex.

"Mae!" he shouted as I pushed open the entrance door. He jogged up the path to me and I couldn't help sighing in appreciation at the way his chest moved under the material of his shirt, making my stomach flutter with excitement.

Shit! Down, you damn hormones!

He reached me and smiled, a small blush covering his cheeks. I couldn't help but smile back at his nervousness. "I uhh…" He swallowed and I had to hold back the 'aww' I wanted to voice at his anxiety. "I would really like to take you to dinner, Mae. If… if that would be okay?"

Dinner? Who the fuck said dinner nowadays?

"In fact, even better, I'd like you to sample my salmon linguine."

I couldn't help but beam at him. He was really trying hard to steal that little something, his eagerness and hope fluttered across his features. "I'd like that very much, thank you."

He exhaled heavily and returned my wide smile. "Brilliant."

I chuckled as his face lit up like a school boy's on snow days. I nodded as I pushed at the door again but he remained frozen to the spot as if his nerves had rendered him immobile. "Okay?"

"Yep." He grinned back as he shook his head and walked away. "Oh, uhh, I'll pick you up at seven, is that okay?"

"Perfect."

"Okay." He grinned again, causing me to laugh loudly. "Right, tomorrow at seven." He nodded as if confirming it to himself before he disappeared around the corner of the street.

I smiled to myself as I pushed through the door, and then cringed as the smell of piss and weed assaulted my nostrils. I sighed, suddenly wishing the place would collapse; it would make it a damn sight prettier.

I huffed as I changed into my fourth outfit. The red off-the-shoulder top and tight jeans staring back at me in the mirror screamed slut and I didn't want to give him the wrong idea, although I had needed to tell myself that same statement over the last hour. My nerves were wrecked which was highly unusual for me, but there was something about Daniel that made my blood heat and my belly clench. He was just male rawness but had such a sweet side that made my heart beat a little quicker.

I narrowed my eyes at myself as I chastised my thoughts. A car door slammed outside and I ran to the window, pulling back the netting. Daniel climbed from a sleek car and smiled up at me staring through the window.

Shit, I didn't want him to enter the foyer; the smell would knock him out before I got to taste those lips.

For Christ's sake, Mae!

I cursed myself, now not having the time to change my slutty top, and snatched up my bag before bounding down the stairs.

As I pushed open the outside door, Daniel gasped and widened his eyes in shock at my sudden appearance. "Holy shit." He chuckled when he noticed my panting. "You're more eager than me."

"I'm just starving." I took his elbow and led him away from the building.

He nodded and opened his passenger door for me to slide in. "It's a good job I have everything prepared then." He walked around the car and climbed in beside me. "We wouldn't want you to be *hungry* for too long," he whispered as he leaned across the car and brushed at a feral strand of hair on top of my head.

My breath stuttered at the way he said hungry. "No," I said simply as I pulled on my seat belt.

I saw him smirk from the corner of my eye as he pulled away.

We were quiet for the journey but I gasped as he pulled up to some huge gates and stabbed a code into a numbered keypad. He seemed angry as he fingered his frustration on the pad; his annoyance making him hit the wrong numbers and causing him to repeat the code three times. "Is everything okay?"

He paused before turning to me, as though he was planting a smile on his face before turning around. "I'm fine, just a little nervous."

His openness squeezed at my heart and I placed my hand on his arm, appreciating the hard muscle beneath my touch. "Don't be nervous, it's just me." I leaned a little further into him. "And I'll eat *anything*."

My eyes widened when I realised how brazen I was being. Daniel's eyes seemed to liquefy before me, the deep brown morphing into a pool of black marble. His teeth nipped at his lips, moistening them until they glistened.

We both blinked when the gates swung open but he remained stock-still, watching me. I wasn't sure if he was angry, horny or just wary. I suddenly wished I could read him better as my nerves flipped a little.

"I presume by that you mean salmon, Mae?"

He seemed to be reprimanding me, scolding me for my audacious comment. I dropped my eyes and swallowed but gave him a nod.

He laughed, taking hold of my hand. "Relax, I'm just teasing you."

I forced a smile and nodded back to him, however there was still a darkness in his eyes that told me very clearly that he hadn't been teasing at all, in fact, far from it.

He smiled again before he let go of my hand and pulled the car up the large gravelled driveway.

"This is just... Wow!" I stuttered. All earlier apprehension disappeared with the beauty welcoming me to Daniel's home. "You live here?"

"Yes. I wouldn't be bringing you here if I didn't, would I?"

Okay, now I was starting to get a little wary of him. Was he calling me stupid or was he just teasing again?

I glanced at him cautiously but rolled my eyes when he winked at me. "You have a weird sense of humour." I smiled. "You take some getting used to, sorry."

He shook his head. "I'm sorry. I'll try to remember you don't know me well. All my friends are used to my dryness. It's just that…"

"It's just what?"

His cheeks flamed brightly as he dropped his eyes to his lap. "Well, it's weird but I feel like I've known you for ages, as though we're already friends and you get me."

He could be so sweet that all my nerves vanished and I smiled at him before climbing from the car. "Just… wow. Your home is stunning."

He didn't answer as he ran up the few steps to the front door. I skimmed my eyes across the lush green garden. It was immaculate; the landscaping took my breath away with the vast array of colours and beautifully shaped shrubs.

The house was maybe a couple of decades old, most definitely modern. The exterior walls were whitewashed but very well maintained and the many windows were all adorned with shutters to give the illusion of a tropical sanctuary.

I reached Daniel on the porch, my eyes still drinking in the grandeur of my surroundings. He cursed under his breath as he flicked through an immense amount of keys on a key-ring. He tried three keys, each time huffing loudly when he rammed another key into the lock that didn't house any of his choices. He finally found the correct one and the door swung open.

He turned to look at me sheepishly. "Sorry. I had the locks changed yesterday and I'm still struggling to find the right key."

He didn't wait for me to answer as he stepped into the hallway. I followed him, somewhat timidly as my eyes widened on the interior. "Holy shit!"

Daniel's head snapped round.

"Sorry."

"I would prefer it if you didn't use such language, Mae."

I swallowed back a laugh. Shit, this man had no clue who I was. I could curse and drink with the sailors on the high seas. Hell, even pirates would welcome me into their fold after spending an hour drinking with me.

His face showed every inch of his disgust and I cringed, the laugh dying in my throat. He stepped towards me, his hand reaching my shoulder before his fingers softly stroked the curve between my neck and shoulder blade. "You are an exquisite, feminine creature, Mae. You should really refrain from trying to hide that side of you."

Okay. What the fuck?

I suddenly didn't want to be there, small bubbles of fear were causing dots of sweat to break over my skin. It wasn't just Daniel's intense dialogue that made me wary but his whole demeanour. The way his eyes fired as they narrowed on me, the way his back stiffened so straight I was concerned for his posture, and the way his teeth gnawed savagely at his lower lip like he was struggling to keep his anger under control.

"Uhh, sorry. That's just me, Daniel." His fingers caused me to shiver as they trailed along my bare shoulder where my top had drooped over the top of my arm. "M...maybe..." I hated that I had started to stutter, I wanted to assert confidence. "Maybe we could take a walk through t...the gardens. They look so beautiful."

Oh Christ.

A tiny moan rumbled up my throat when Daniel's lips brushed across the curve of my shoulder. An intense heat shimmied up my legs from my toes and crashed into my womb with a raw power I had never experienced before.

I jumped a mile when the door slammed shut behind me.

"But why, Mae?" He leaned back until his eyes were on my face again. "You obviously came here to be fucked. That top you're wearing screams that you are hoping it gets ripped the fuck off you tonight."

My knees wobbled. It wasn't just his words; they weren't said as though to a lover in a passionate moment. They were filled with revulsion and aggression.

"The way your jeans display the tight contours of your backside." He sneered as I took a step back and he took one forward. "You are flaunting your curves,

Mae. You wanted to look hot for me so I would fuck you, didn't you?"

I took another step back as his face contorted angrily. His lip curled at the corner with his abhorrence, his eyes darkened as hatred reflected back at me. "DIDN'T YOU?"

I shook my head as I continued to move backwards, but he kept coming. He kept placing one foot in front of the other, he kept the threatening sneer on his face, and he kept his gaze full of ire.

I knew then, before I took another step that that night... I would lose something I had struggled to hold onto for so long. Something that was going to be taken from me even if I tried with everything I had to hold on tight.

But I wouldn't go down without a fight.

I spun round and within milliseconds soaked up my surroundings then headed for the patio doors situated on the rear wall of the room. He was right behind me, his loud, sinister laugh eating up the air around me as I retained whatever my lungs held and converted the oxygen to adrenaline.

"Oh, Mae." He tutted as I yanked at the door, cursing when it remained lodged in the framework. "You underestimate me."

I shot off to the right and headed down a long corridor; doors appeared left and right but I bypassed them, knowing they would just be rooms he could trap me in. The hallway veered off to the left and I slid around the corner, hissing at the sharp pain that burst in my calf and fired needles through my leg.

"Fuck!" My leg gave way and I jolted, causing me to lose a few yards gap between us.

"Oh, I love a chase," he sniggered when he'd almost caught up with me.

I fisted a door at the end of the hall. To my utter surprise it popped open and I surged forward.

A huge pool greeted me but I didn't have chance to appreciate its tranquillity. All I saw were the doors to the garden at the other side of the room.

"Keep running, Mae. You have a rare spirit that I rather like," he mocked as he gained on me, his words driving more determination in me to win this stupid fucking game. I couldn't let him win. I *wouldn't* let him win.

I cheered inwardly as I reached the door and it opened, the gust of night air hitting my face and clinging to the sweat that poured from me. The outside world had never looked so fucking heartening and the adrenaline rushing through my veins doubled as I pushed harder and charged forward.

You know afterwards, when you replay things over in your mind? Well for me, for the next three years, all I could concentrate on was the twisted muscle in my calf that had slowed me down. All I could tell myself for three years was, if I hadn't slid around the corner, if I had taken it at a practical speed and not acted like a fucking athlete at the Olympics, then maybe, just maybe I would have gotten away that night with my virginity intact.

I remember the sinking in my heart, the dread that slithered through every fibre in me when his hand snatched at my hair and I was slung around so forcefully I slid along the tiled floor a few feet and came to rest at the edge of the pool.

I scrambled around and pushed myself to all fours. A loud scream burst from me when Daniel's shoe connected with the base of my spine and the most torturous pain fired up my vertebrae. "So pointless, little lamb. Why fight it? I know you will be wet when I take you."

Through the humiliation, the pain, the dread and the fear, it was his little pet name that gave me the sickening feeling. As he slid his foot up my back, the reality of what he was came at me like a lightning bolt, illuminating the foolish parts of my brain and allowing me to see the full picture clearly. He was a professional. The small blushes as he had played with my compassionate side, the soft smiles as he had appealed to my sensual side and the knight in shining armour act that had guaranteed my trust.

"Please don't do this." I hated myself for begging, for giving this sick bastard what he would expect but I couldn't help it. It was human nature, defensive instinct to plead with someone's humanity.

"Get up."

I ignored him, choosing to bury myself further into the cold ceramic floor. Chlorine from the pool assaulted my nostrils, making my eyes water and my lungs hiss with the chemical rush.

I cried out as he yanked me upright by my hair, his fingers twisting the length in his hold until it snatched at my scalp and made my temples burn. He jerked my head until my face was an inch from his.

"Now, I'm going to make this simple for you, Mae. Meet my demands with perfection and this will be a lot easier. Fight me, disobey my orders, then you will need to be aware that I will take your obstinacy as a direct request for punishment. Do you understand me?"

I stared at him. My jaw was locked; my throat was constricted to an extent that it refused anything including air to escape, and my mouth had dried up to the degree that my tongue had swollen.

He shook me hard, a deep red tint seeping onto his pale face with fury at my silence. "Do – you – understand – me?"

I nodded but didn't answer, causing him to narrow his eyes. "Speak!"

I blinked at him but managed to choke out a yes with another nod of my head.

"Good." He let go of my hair and watched me closely. "Take off your clothes."

"No!" I shook my head furiously, my instincts still fighting the bastard all the way. Fuck him and his *punishment*. Fuck him and his *demands*! I was built to fight, my mind moulded to deny any submission. If he wanted me then I wasn't about to make it easy for him. I was created to conflict anything hostile, therefore making this not just harder on myself but, almost gleefully, a lot more challenging for him.

The light disappeared as my body crashed into the water, the slap against the surface stung my back even through the material of my top. It was warm and almost pleasurable, its comfort embracing me and soothing my body slightly. I surfaced and coughed, spluttering on the little water that had managed to trickle into my lungs. My eyes tingled with the chemicals in the water as I pushed my hair from my face.

"I warned you, Mae. Now you've just made this a whole lot more stimulating. I repeat, take – off – your – clothes."

"No!"

I pushed back and started to swim across the water, my arms aching as the fear coursing through me swallowed up my adrenaline. Although I was usually a good swimmer, I wasn't world class but I wasn't an amateur, the panic riding me made the task torturous and gruelling, my muscles appealing with me to give up and grant them respite.

I palmed the edge of the pool and pushed myself up. Fingers curled around my ankle and pulled me back. I hadn't heard or felt him slip into the water behind me. As he tugged my leg, his other hand pressed down on the top of my head until I was completely underwater; his sheer strength held me exactly where he wanted me, a few inches below the surface.

I grappled with him as the oxygen rapidly depleted from my lungs. I hadn't managed to take much of a breath before he'd plunged me under and my lungs struggled at the withdrawal of their stimulant. I kicked at him as a haze surrounded my vision and an almighty burn blistered my nostrils and throat.

He didn't relent, his firm grip rendering me powerless under him as he showed me exactly who was boss.

My lungs heaved in vast amounts of air when he removed his hand and dragged me to the surface. The noises my throat emitted were somewhat embarrassing, well they would have been if I had given a damn about what Daniel thought of me.

"Next time, I promise I will not grant you another lifeline. The next time you disobey, you will die." He was so blunt and carefree with his statement that I knew he would keep his word.

I nodded in defeat, hating myself for submitting but acknowledging that if I wanted to live there was nothing more to be done.

"Now, once more. Remove your slutty clothes."

I lowered my face, not wanting to see the victory in his eyes as I tugged off my top. The weight of the water made my efforts slow and difficult but I managed to pull it off and kept my gaze on the red material as it sunk slowly to the bottom of the pool whilst I dragged at the wet denim covering my legs.

I wouldn't describe what I felt as humiliation when my nudity was exposed to him; it was more of a deep sorrow. All that raced around my thoughts was that the first man to ever see me naked since my father was a man who I could have fallen in love with. Daniel's gentility and attentiveness had appealed to me, had made me realise exactly what I was looking for. He had been my ideal, a man I could have spent long nights making love to, a man I could have given my soul to, but he took both those ideals and turned them into something evil and sordid, twisting my hopes and dreams into something cruel and mocking.

"Look at me, little lamb."

I lifted my head but fixed my gaze on the wall behind his shoulder, still refusing him all of my surrender. He pinched my chin between his fingers and slowly directed my face until I was looking straight into his eyes. "I am the sort of man who will relish in your defiance, Mae. Believe me, I would love nothing more than to fight you, to take you hard and punishingly, to bruise you and make you bleed. But I'll admit there's something about you that I like so I'm willing to make this easy for you."

The way he spoke brought on a warm glow, a relief that he liked me. His acceptance made my belly flutter.

It was this realisation that made me spin my head and vomit on the surface of the water. How could a monster bring out these feelings of need and want? How could someone who was about to hurt me make me crave his acceptance and then bask in the small amount of praise he gave me?

Nausea and anger brought my tears as I finally submitted and let him take what he wanted. I wasn't worthy of any more anyway; the way I had delighted in his approval made me as sick as him.

He sighed as though disappointed in me before he told me to climb out and stand facing the wall.

I did as he asked without hesitation or argument. I had given in, completely handed myself over to him.

Whether it was instinct that took away my fight or whether my brain realised it was this or die, I wasn't sure, but I abandoned any hope that this was all a mistake and I would be leaving there with my soul unbroken.

"See how easy it is? How simple this whole thing will pass if you obey?"

I nodded. I knew it was expected as I murmured a yes to accompany the gesture. I could feel his breath on the back of my neck, the heat from him trickling across my wet skin as a shiver ravaged my body. "Now bend forward and palm the wall."

I closed my eyes and slid my hands along the cool tiles, concentrating on the texture of the smooth surface.

A solitary tear slipped from the corner of my eye as Daniel took my innocence in a single thrust. I never felt the pain of losing my virginity, all I experienced was an overwhelming numbness that rolled over me like a mist across the morning tide. A detachment surrounded me as his fingers curled around my hips and he began to groan.

It's funny how you think you'll react when being raped. I'm not sure how other people saw it but I always imagined I'd scream and cry and fight, but in the moment, in the actual moment that a man took away my soul, I felt nothing.

I closed my eyes as another tear leaked from me, just a sole one, a lonely one that craved the comfort of its partner and chased it down my face quickly as it tried to gain solace from its mate. I wanted to catch it on my finger before it dripped off my chin and abandoned me. I needed it to remain with me; the only sensation I could feel was its trickle down my face and I had an overwhelming feeling that when it managed to leave me, it would take the remaining parts of my spirit with it.

But it didn't hear my pleas; it didn't wait to see the massacre unfold as it fell from my face and splashed on the floor by my little toe.

My mother's smile comforted me as Daniel thrust harder and clawed at my back, his nails scraping the skin on either side of my spinal column as he grew feverish and animalistic. I was flung around. My knees crashed on the hard floor as a hand pushed my head down until I was completely flat against the floor, my cheek squashed against the unforgiving coldness of the floor tiles. Yet, still I remained unfeeling and disconnected.

Comfort came in the image of my mother's beautiful smile and happy eyes as she took my hand and led me across the field. The swallows were out, their silhouettes gliding against the sunlight, providing shadows to dance across the strip of sunlight marking our path through the trees. Their song was a pretty one, as though they welcomed me and my mother to their home, their happy calls of pride in their habitat brought my mother's laughter.

Another tear fell as I felt him become more frenzied. Yule, our three-year-old Scotty dog, bounced after a stick my mom threw, his tail swishing happily as he chased and fetched. I laughed when he leapt after a squirrel and dived straight into the stream. He had never been a good judge of his surroundings, his constant knocks and grazes against all things in his path had been the bane of my parents' life with expensive vet bills, but their love for Yule had seen them fork out hundreds after hundreds.

I started to sing with my dead Mother as she grinned happily at me. *Somewhere over the Rainbow* filled my thoughts, taking my attention as my hand swung in hers and we giggled and sang louder. The swallows scurried away, making us laugh harder as we scared them with our singing.

I started to lose consciousness when something was slipped into my mouth, an old rag or some sort of towel stuffed between my open jaws. I groaned when I eventually felt something. There was a mass of wetness between my legs that felt warm and almost obstructive. The sensation made me shiver as revulsion coiled in my gut.

"Oh dear, and I said I wouldn't make you bleed." Daniel's voice fluttered around in my head but the haze unfocussed the meaning of his words and I continued to stare at the small crack in one of the tiles on the wall.

I didn't feel him finish, or pull out. I didn't even feel the pull of sleep after he slid a needle into my vein. All I felt was the overwhelming warmth of motherly comfort I had missed for over four years.

She had always been there through my childhood scrapes and calamities, had always soothed me and mopped up my tears. She had always shown me where to find my courage, how to dig deep inside me and pull up the nerve to deal with life's hell.

And even though she left me four years ago with my father in a fatal car accident, she had remained true and returned to help me through the most horrific hell I could face.

It would be another three years before I saw her again, but this time she would be taking me back, as should be, mother and daughter together.

Chapter Three

'Do not pity yourself, others will do that.'

Aged 21

I smirked to myself as I circled the spoon in my coffee, the pattern it made deeply mesmerising. The couple at the opposite table had been arguing for over twenty minutes. Apparently she wanted to buy her mother a Kindle for Christmas; he said they were way too expensive, around thirty pounds more than he wanted to spend on her. So then she said the photo shoot he wanted to arrange for his mother could take a swim in the canal because that was around forty pounds more than a Kindle.

Thank God I would be buying just one gift this year - the semi-expensive bottle of wine I always treated myself to when watching It's *A Wonderful Life*.

I turned my gaze away from them and sighed as I saw the first snow of the year collect on the bottom edge of the windowsill. I hated snow with a passion. I'd fallen on the damn stuff when I was around nine and broke my arm, a week before the gymnastics tournament I'd had a good chance of winning.

Numerous couples strolled past, each carrying a vast array of gift bags and treats for the holiday period, their bonuses from the yearly toil at work providing them with the luxury of what Christmas was.

High powered businessmen rushed into jewellers to buy last minute expensive offerings for their wives that would get them laid for the first time since their birthday in the summer. Giggling children looked to the sky, each opening their mouths eagerly to catch as many flakes as possible as the many festive lights in the store windows danced across their faces, lighting them up even more than their own excitement.

I smiled and wiggled my fingers at a little girl, no more than four, who stared at me through the window, her hand holding tightly onto her mother's, who was currently discussing the latest gossip with a friend she hadn't seen for a week.

Her lips twitched nervously before the small smile grew into a grin and she waved back hesitantly. Her mother looked down then turned to see what had caught her daughter's attention. She narrowed her eyes then pulled the little girl round to the front of her and out of view.

I sighed sadly as the window reflected to me what the mother had seen. I quickly turned back to the interior of the café, hiding myself from both the public and myself.

John, one of the waiters who worked in the small café I always frequented, smiled sadly at me then winked. I hated his pity, hated the way he would give me the biggest pastry or how he would often slide me an extra coffee when his boss was in the back. Yet I smiled back, as always, before I stood and pulled on my coat, slipping my scarf around my neck and tugging on my gloves.

"See ya tomorrow, Mae," John called to me as I headed towards the door.

I smiled and lifted my hand to him, ignoring the way his eyes roved over my coat and then down to my backside. I needed a new coat, one that preferably covered my backside.

The cold bit at my face when I stepped into the street, the ice that already covered the pavement made my feet skid in my cheap shoes and my hand shot out to grab onto the lamppost.

"Whoa, steady."

I turned to the voice as hands shot around my waist to halt my fall. "Thank you." I smiled appreciatively at the man as he held on to me tightly.

His smile dropped and he nodded quickly before he let me go and walked off hurriedly, his own feet skidding in his haste to get away from the monster. I stared after him, insensitive to his reaction. I was hardened to their responses when they saw me, detachment and disinterest being a blessed emotion.

The walk home took longer than the usual fifteen minutes as my attention was sucked in by all the glorious pieces in each of the huge department store windows. Pretty cocktail dresses in pinks, blues and creams dressed pretty mannequins in one, delicate glistening jewelled necklaces on an assortment of shelves decorated another window but it was always the final window that stole my breath and formed many of my dreams. The beautiful wedding dress that hung from the model in the window was the most exquisite thing I'd ever seen. It hugged the sculpture perfectly, the soft cream lace draping dreamily as the tiny diamante butterflies embedded into the fine silk of the skirt twinkled with the shop lights. The pretty sweetheart neckline was complimented with the most beautiful blue diamond that hung from a platinum chain and rested precisely at the base of her throat.

The male mannequin was dressed in the finest suit, expensive and stylish, as he rested on one knee before the lady, holding her hand as he slipped a ring onto her finger.

Rose petals and white blossom littered the floor around their feet as various lights sparkled in the floor, giving the scene a fairy-tale aspect.

I ran my finger over the window, the wool of my gloves scratching at the ice that had formed as I traced around the love heart that had been painted onto the window. I sighed as I read the passage on the prop board behind the happy couple, *'Love is made from dreams, and dreams are made of love'*.

That's all mine would ever be, dreams. My hopes were just dreams, my future just a dream made up from the nightmares of my past.

I knew this scene before me would never belong to me; that was why it seemed to embrace me as it simultaneously taunted me. It gave me something to dream of when I had plenty of horrors to keep me awake at night.

No man would ever look at me the way this artificial man looked at his love, the way his eyes idolised his bride, the way his dreams all featured his pretty wife.

I was too ugly to be idolised, inside and out. I had made sure of both. I had made sure that no man would ever look at me and desire me.

I had created a monster that would repel the Devil himself.

"Going to Bert's?" Spud asked as I punched my card out the next afternoon. I nodded without looking at him. "I'll walk with ya. I need to nip in Theo's for a gift for Theresa."

I quirked an eyebrow and finally looked at him. "Spud, its Christmas Eve. Are you telling me you haven't bought your wife's present yet?"

He shrugged. "Haven't had the money 'til today. I was hoping on a bonus but..."

"That hope shot you in the leg." I laughed.

Spud and I had worked together in the pizza factory for around two years. He was fun but very childlike, which left me wondering many times how his wife ever coped with him, yet we had hit it off from the start, both of us with the same sense of humour and anger at life. "Mmm, you'd think just one year Tony would push the boat out. I mean it's Christmas and all."

I leaned into him as we pushed out of the factory doors; the late afternoon air was heavy with the promise of more snow. "I'll let you into a secret about Tony's wealth." I told him quietly. "Tony is rich. Humungously rich. And the reason for that is because he doesn't give his petty workers a Christmas bonus. Instead he spends that horde of cash on prostitutes, slaves and golf clubs."

Spud nodded slowly. "Ahh, and here was me thinking he just hated us."

I chuckled and nudged him with my elbow as we reached the door to Bert's café. "How can he hate us? We're the pepperoni and cheese on his pizza."

He smiled at me and slid his arm around my waist to give me a brotherly hug, his lips quickly pecking the top of my head. "And it's about time you were the pepperoni and cheese to someone else's pizza, Mae."

I rolled my eyes and huffed at him. "Uh-uh, big guy. You know the rules. You do not discuss my love life in public, nor do you even mention it between the two of us."

"Oh come on, Mae. You're perfect. What isn't to love?"

I twisted my lips and fought a smile as I pointed a finger at my face. "Umm, I really hope Theresa bought you some glasses this year. Seems you're having trouble seeing properly."

He scowled at me which was usual for our traditional conversation over my life. "Fuck that, Mae. Your inner beauty is what makes you the special person you are. You are stunning. Your huge eyes, bloody hell, even Theresa is jealous of those. The way your lips pout naturally makes you a stunner, and those bloody sculptured cheekbones... fuck... hot, Mae."

I stared at him then let out the laughter. "Shit, Spud, don't let your wife hear you say those things. Sounds like you have a bit of a thing for me." I knew he was just trying to be nice and his heart was all there but to be told you're beautiful by someone who's practically your brother doesn't have the same effect.

I reached up and placed a tender kiss on his cheek. "You have a good Christmas, Spud. I'll see you in the new year."

He smiled then let out a deep sigh. The sadness in his eyes descended quickly but he shifted it when he saw my reaction. "Well, if you change your mind about Christmas dinner you know Theresa and I would love to have you."

"I know." I smiled widely, thankful for his friendship and care. "But I'll be fine. Me and the TV have a hot date... oh and the bottle of Chardonnay that has my name on it."

He nodded once then wrapped me up in his arms. The wool from his coat itched at my nose but I held on as tight as he did, relishing in his companionship and affection. It would be the last I saw of him until the factory opened up again after the Christmas break. "Well, Mae Swift. Happy Christmas, darling. I really hope this one grants you your dreams," he whispered before he was gone, leaving me holding the door to Bert's open, furious shouts of *'its freezing, shut the damn door'* echoing around me.

I stood behind the man in the long grey coat already ordering coffee at the counter as I pulled my purse from my bag. I flicked through the coins and sighed.

"Usual, Mae?" John shouted over the shoulder of the man to me.

"Just coffee today, John, thanks."

He scowled at me as I counted the right change and placed it on the counter then went over to my usual table by the window and settled to people watch.

I unwrapped my scarf from around my neck and pulled off my gloves, flicking my gaze over the outside world of shoppers, commuters, and just Sheffield in general. The tram slid past and I smiled to myself. Everything was as it should be. The 5:15 commute from Meadowhall to Sheffield central was running on time. Bob, who ran the small hardware shop across the road, lifted his hand to me before he brought in his shop sign. Mavis from the florists smiled and waved as she slid into her beat up Punto. And John placed my double shot, white coffee on the table in front of me – with my favourite cherry lattice pastry. I scowled at him. He winked before he went back to see to the other customers.

I ripped the corner of the sugar packet and poured the brown contents into my coffee then picked up the spoon to stir. The spoon clanged against the cup when each single hair on my body rose in awareness, ice trickled along my spine as my muscles seized up in fear.

I spun round in my chair, my eyes furiously scanning my surroundings to see what had set my instincts on high alert. The usual regulars carried on with their conversations. John and Bert laughed at something playing on the cheap TV that was housed on the precarious shelf at the back of the workspace. The snow continued to pile up outside, but there was something off, something that had my heart racing and my throat closing in.

"Hi, Mae," a voice shouted from the other side of the café. Before turning I glanced again through the window, desperately trying to spot what had the attention of my sixth sense. A shadow moved through the tiny alleyway beside Mavis', a tall silhouette with a masculine frame and gait, his long grey overcoat blew out behind him as he hurried around the corner.

"Mae?"

I jolted and whirled to see Shirley grinning at me with her crooked yellow teeth, the many strands of hair that jutted from her chin causing me to shudder. "Sorry, Shirley. I was miles away."

"That you were, my dear. Anywhere nice?"

"Not really." I grimaced and scanned the room for the guy who had been in front of me at the counter queue. "Did you see a man in here, Shirley?"

She lifted her eyebrows then laughed, her manic cackle reminding me very much of the witch she also resembled in appearances. "I see lots of men, lovey."

I quirked a brow back at her but she winked and patted my shoulder. She fixed her eyes then tilted her head curiously and snatched her hand back from me as though my shoulder had shocked her. She gasped and held a hand to her chest. "Oh my."

"Okay, Shirley." I peered at her hesitantly. "Way to go on the freaky shit."

She blinked but shook her head as she continued to scrutinise me. "I..." She shook her head again then turned and walked off, sitting herself back in her seat at her regular table in the other corner of the room. Her eyes fixed on me, her odd stare penetrating me for the whole duration of my time spent there.

I purposely ignored Shirley as I hurried through my cherry Danish and coffee, my eyes roaming the street outside the entire time. Nothing seemed unusual, yet I couldn't help but wind myself up. The anguish and fear raged through my veins, building the pressure in my head until I felt like I would explode.

The fifteen minutes journey home took a record ten minutes as my little legs hurried along the three streets to my apartment, my eyes glancing in every direction as my head turned left and right to check for any company and my ears were open to the slightest noise around me.

The build-up of pressure was becoming unbearable as every fibre in me throbbed mercilessly and my brain thumped against my temples. The incessant bang, bang, bang made my teeth grind against each other as my stomach coiled with fear.

The kids on the estate gave me their usual welcome home as they greeted me with taunts and pelted handfuls of ice that scratched my cheeks and lips, one particular chip cutting an inch of skin above my right eye, it's deep gash actually doing me a favour and giving me enough of a reprieve against the pain to get me to my apartment. To them I wasn't Mae Swift, the pizza maker whose life was hanging in the balance. No, I was the ugly freak, the weird girl who lived on the ground floor in apartment 4 who never had company, never made a connection with any of them or even looked their way, the hideous scarred weirdo who provided them with entertainment on a housing estate that didn't offer any other source of amusement.

I shoved my front door closed behind me, placing the four chains in their housings, sliding the lock into place and slipping the three bolts into their catches.

I flicked every single light on my journey through my apartment, obliterating the shadows that threatened to choke me as I worked my way through to my bedroom. I dropped to my knees in front of the wardrobe and dug my hands under the blankets at the bottom, feeling for what I wanted.

As soon as the small tin found my fingers I sighed as release was suddenly realistic and not held just beyond reach.

I dashed into the bathroom, finally flicking the little pull cord that operated the little strobe light above the sink and pulled open my battered little tin. The contents fell into the sink in my haste but I didn't care, it made it easier to find what I wanted.

I grabbed at the button on my jeans, ready to pull them off before I realised I wouldn't be seen in public for over a week and didn't need to hide.

I yanked off my coat and tore at my sleeve until it was rolled above my elbow.

My shoulders sagged, my brain sighed and my veins tingled in ecstasy at the first stroke of the blade across the underside of my forearm. My vision swam in delight as I watched the bubbles of blood surface against the paleness of my skin.

My whole body relaxed, my chest unwound, and a deep tranquillity flowed through me with the second pull of the razor against my tight flesh. My heart started to slow back to its regular beat as my chest slowly rose and fell. A heavy sigh vibrated through me, my veins now allowing my blood to flow uninhibited around my body as the constriction eased.

I opened the mirrored cabinet above the sink and hunted for the cotton balls I knew were in there. I moved things around when they didn't show up.

"Strange, I could've sworn..."

My whole life ended when I closed the cupboard door. My heart stopped as a whooshing noise echoed in my ears and my stomach actually gurgled when the acid in it ate the fear that filled it. It seemed too surreal to be real. I was dreaming, that was all; maybe I had banged my head without realising on the way home.

The reflection in the mirror showed the blood leave my face, the flush in my cheeks disappearing as another face materialised over my shoulder.

His mouth twisted into a sinister grin as his threatening chocolate eyes darkened. "Hello again, little lamb."

Chapter Four

'Accept the pain. Fear the agony.'

The door opened. I didn't have the energy to turn myself towards the light that streaked into the room; I simply closed my eyes to it.

I heard the slow plod of his heavy feet on the concrete floor, however I no longer feared him. Fear wouldn't save me, it wouldn't end this nightmare. Fear was of no use to me now. I was too exhausted. I just wanted a reprieve from life. I wanted him to get it over with and end it.

The twitch in my big toe was back, the strain from being suspended for so long with just the soles of my feet softly touching the floor causing the slight imbalance in my nerve endings and strain to my muscles.

My legs ached from my shins to my thighs and a fierce burn in my calves ate at my muscles. My arms were numb, my fingers no longer belonging to me but to the chain they had been curled around for so long they had set, giving me an almost garden sculpture resemblance. I had laughed at that thought, many hours ago, the thought that I'd actually die attached to a chain with my fingers seeking support from the thing that caused their pain, my grip so tight I had become one with the metal.

Footsteps circled around me, their slow pace rhythmic and calming after the long silence, their thud, thud, thud sending me into a conscious unconsciousness. His breaths were heavy and loud, regular and paced precisely as he inhaled through his nose then exhaled through his mouth. It was amazing what your senses picked up after a deep quiet.

He moved away, the bump of his feet growing softer the further he got. I tried to regulate my breathing to the pattern of his movement, inhaling or exhaling every time his foot connected with the ground but his steps were a tad quicker than my shallow breathing.

I was suddenly dropped, my body screamed out at the sudden release, my muscles shrivelling and my bones cracking with the abrupt action. The side of my head bounced off the concrete, my neck unable to support it as my body sagged to the floor. Pain shot to every single section of my body, the knock causing me to cry out as I tried to lift my hands to cradle my head, but the muscles in my arms were too weak.

"Nadu, Mae."

I fought with the heaviness of my eyelids but the effort was too strenuous. He repeated himself and I prised my eyes open, the harshness of the light in the room piercing my brain and stinging my eyes.

I winced unconsciously when he dropped to his haunches before me, his forearms on his thighs as he studied me intensely.

"You have a lot to learn, Mae," he said, his tone calm but controlled. I stared at him, unable to give him any response. "But you will," he finished with a sigh before he stood back up and tilted his head as though waiting for something. "Let's make this simpler for you."

I squealed when he bent and gripped my hair then yanked me upright, my legs splayed out by the side of me as he supported my weary body with his hold. "When I enter, you will kneel with your knees apart and your hands on your thighs. Do you understand?"

I squinted, bewilderment and confusion now an enemy when his words jumbled in my head. I shook my head as much as I could. Why the fuck would he want me to kneel?

He sighed faintly and pulled on my hair, lifting me further off the ground as pain shot through my scalp and into my brain. I yelped when he kicked at my legs. Instinct drew them into my body as I tried to tuck them underneath me to protect them.

He tutted and sighed when I obviously didn't meet his satisfaction. "Look at me, Mae."

I blinked furiously when my eyes still refused to accommodate the light, the pain torturing me until I gave in and left them closed. I cried out when the back of his hand shot across my cheek, firing a deep burn through the flesh as my head knocked against the ground once more.

"Look – at – me."

I squeezed my eyes shut then attempted to open them, furiously trying to ignore the pain and focus on him.

"Better." He pulled in a breath and crouched low again, his hard eyes on mine, daring me to close them again. I whimpered when he lifted up a bottle of water and waggled it in his fingers. "You want this, lamb? Are you thirsty?"

I gave him a simple nod as I begged him with my eyes.

"Speak."

I swallowed against the dryness and clog in my throat that had settled there hours ago. "Yes," I managed to croak out, gulping again at the soreness in my throat.

"Then kneel."

I stared at him for a moment, checking for any humour on his face but there was none. This man was deadly serious. If I didn't want to die of dehydration then I needed to kneel.

I shifted slowly, palming the floor as I tried to push myself up. My knees screamed at the bent position after being vertical for so long, however I managed to manoeuvre until I resembled some sort of kneeling position before him.

"Chin up."

I sighed in frustration and lifted my face until I was staring straight at him in his crouched position. His eyes pierced mine, the rich brown melting before my eyes as a blaze fired in them. He propped my chin a little higher with a finger until my eyes were on his forehead. "You will never make eye contact with me again."

What was with him? He needn't worry though, I never wanted to look at him again. Those eyes had haunted my nightmares for years.

He stood and slipped a foot between my knees. "Open your legs slightly."

I was too tired and thirsty to argue, in addition to the extreme pain over-ruling every single thought in my head so I did as he asked and shuffled my knees apart. "Further," he whispered. I gulped at the throb that fired in the pit of my gut with his soft tone, fear and terror controlling my blood system and surging dread into every nerve ending with his tender tone.

I sank my teeth into my bottom lip as I held onto my new found temper. It festered inside me, allowing me to nurture it and give me strength. I'd make sure to get the water before he got my wrath.

He took a step back to study me. My eyes closed as humiliation burnt in me. "Open your eyes, Mae. Straighten your back and put your hands on your thighs." His words were clear and meticulous, firing my deep-seated anger higher and higher but I did what he expected, pulling myself into his required pose.

"Better."

He crouched before me again and took hold of my chin, tilting my head back slowly. "Open your mouth, little lamb." His soft tone made me shiver.

Like a lamb to the slaughter.

I gulped at the cool liquid when he held it to my lips and allowed me to drink, the lubrication to my sore throat was nectar but my belly griped angrily.

"Enough," he barked. "Sip it."

I swallowed frequently as he poured small amounts into my mouth but as he removed it, my hand shot up to his to stop his confiscation of my life source. He removed the bottle instantly and grabbed onto my wrist tightly. He didn't speak, just glared at me with hatred. "EYES!" he snapped when I looked at him.

I dropped my gaze to the floor and waited. His breathing calmed and I relaxed a little. His expensive shoes reflected the curl of my lip as he unlocked my wrists from the cuffs. "Get up."

I rolled my eyes at the floor and pushed myself upright, finally planting my feet solidly on the floor after three attempts. I stood straight as his gaze wondered over my filthy body. "Follow me."

I shuffled after him as he walked from the room. He was pacing ahead but my eyes were too busy taking in my surroundings to take much notice of him.

"Holy shittin' fuck," I breathed as I stared at the luxury around that poxy little shithole he had kept me in.

I screamed out as his knuckles connected with my mouth and I fell against the banister. "Keep your filthy mouth closed from now on."

I gasped and brought my hand to my mouth, dabbing gently at my lip. Blood covered it when I brought it away. Fury bubbled inside me, its strength overpowering me as I launched myself at him. Instinct took control of my temper and gave it sustenance as my fist rocked his head to the side with a sharp snap, his jaw cracking under the force.

He was on me in seconds. My back hit the floor with a sickening thud as his huge body straddled me. He grabbed both of my hands in his single one before he brought his fist into my face four times. My cheek exploded, bringing tears to them as my sore, swollen eyes squeezed shut against his abuse. He grabbed my hair and held my head down as his face came an inch from mine. "You ever touch me again and I will hurt you. You think this is pain?" he spat as I whimpered and cried underneath him. "Then you have a lot to learn about me, Mae. I can crush you in a heartbeat, and believe me, I will."

His spittle sprayed my face as his warm breath clung to the wetness from my tears.

"Fuck you!" I spat back. Impulse urged me to fight back, refuse his dominance. In a way I hoped my challenge would encourage him to finish this, my mind was playing with the scenario too much, feeding me with horrors and fright of what was to come.

His chest heaved as his jaw clenched, his teeth cracking loudly under the power as he got up and dragged me across the floor by my hair. My body felt heavy but he pulled me as though I weighed nothing.

My already bruised frame bounced along the bathroom's porcelain floor tiles before he slung me into the huge shower cubicle. Freezing cold water pelted me, my skin shrinking back at the assault as I gasped for breath and scrambled around on the floor.

He forced my head back with a firm hold on my hair as he directed the jet of water into my mouth. "Let's cleanse that dirty mouth, shall we?"

I squeezed my mouth closed, cutting off his want to drown me but the torrent of water blocked my nose. My mouth opened, causing me to drown again. It was a vicious circle as he refused to let up, the water either suffocating me or drowning me. I was deliberating which of the two would be the best way to go when the water suddenly took on a new horror as the heat suddenly intensified and pelts of scorching water attacked my cold, delicate skin.

I screamed and clambered to the back of the cubicle, protecting my body from the blistering heat as I wrapped my arms around myself.

He shut off the water and stared at me, his head marginally tilted to the side as his eyes burrowed deep inside me. "More?"

I shook my head furiously. "No, please."

I hated the pleading tone in my voice but my body couldn't survive anymore abuse. I was exhausted, in extreme pain and my willpower had fucked off with the water down the drain.

"Nadu!" He barked that stupid word again and I shrugged at him. He closed his eyes, fighting for patience before he snapped them open. "Nadu!" he barked out again. "Kneel, Mae."

"Oh," I whispered as I scrambled around, bringing myself to a kneeling position again.

"Knees," he whispered in that damn tone that liquefied my mind. It fooled my senses and I relaxed marginally in relief.

I shuffled my knees apart slightly and remembered to place my hands on my thighs.

His smile lit my insides, made me sigh as a reprieve in his anger gave my mind a moment's peace, and a small jolt of happiness jerked my lips upwards into a tiny, proud smile.

"Very good," he praised with a small nod. "Now wash yourself."

I blinked at him but shifted quickly when he reached for the shower controls. "Yes," I answered as I adjusted the temperature and switched the water back on.

His hand shot out to stop me when I started to pull at the glass door. He shook his head slowly then went to settle in the chair that was facing the cubicle. He sat back and crossed one leg over the other as he clasped his fingers together and rested them in his lap.

"You want me to shower on my knees?" I gasped him with a look of bewilderment. Darkness covered his face as an enraged gleam filled his eyes. "I'm sorry," I bit out as I held my hands up and picked up the soap.

I hated my reticence, hated how I submitted to him so easily but right then I was too tired to argue and fight. I had been fighting the memory of him for the last three years with no success, and to have him a metre from me, his evil once more polluting the air around me was impossible to oppose. He overpowered me with ease, the sheer strength of him pointless to battle with. The knowledge of how cruel he could be suppressed anymore thoughts of denying his orders. He destroyed my life three years ago, not just physically but emotionally and spiritually. I had never gotten over what he did; his actions that day made me question not just my own judgement but the intentions of everyone else around me.

That is what made him so powerful; not the pain he could cause to my body, but the agony he brought to my soul.

However, I would build myself back up then I'd fight the fucker all the way. That was a promise. I once again needed to find the resilient little girl my mother had loved and raised. I needed to rediscover the defiant and strong mind my father had encouraged in me. I had to learn to trust myself and learn how to fight with not just a physical strength, but hard emotion and a tough mind.

His eyes followed the route of my hands as I remained kneeling and washed myself. The expensive soap was luxurious against the filth engrained into my sore skin, the gentle pulse of the warm water soothing to my nerves.

"Wash your pussy, dirty little lamb."

My eyes shot to his but I quickly lowered them and blew out a steadying breath. Oh God damn shittin' fuck - I made sure to say it in my head that time.

I lathered up the soap meticulously, stealing time as I spun it and spun it in my grip, watching it twist and slide in my hands. I shuddered and closed my eyes as I slipped my hands between my legs and scrubbed at my bits quickly.

All done.

I smiled to myself as I hastily rinsed myself and shut off the water.

"Wash yourself again."

"What?" The words rushed from my lips without permission and I almost shrivelled in despair.

He pushed himself upright, his eyes on mine as his teeth chewed his bottom lip again. His slow steps towards me were torturous and my skin prickled as fear gripped me. His fingers circled my neck before he pulled me to stand before him. "Do not ever question me again," he seethed. "I tell you to do something, you do it, no question, no hesitation. You DO IT!"

I jumped and nodded. "I'm sorry."

"Now, wash – your – dirty – cunt – again."

I nodded and restarted the water, already soaping my hands. He stood close, watching me as I closed my eyes and drew my hands between my legs. "Look at me," he whispered.

My stomach rolled. What the hell was with that bloody pitch in his voice that affected me like it did? I hated it, I hated the way it made me feel. I hated him. Yet that soft tone made my body want to comply and gave my mind some sort of ease. It relaxed me because right at that very second he was calm and in control, it meant he was pleased with me and wouldn't use violence to manage me.

He sighed heavily and I shot my eyes to his before he reacted to my hesitation. He held my gaze as I washed myself, his chest rising and falling heavily.

His eyes finally dropped to watch my cleaning. Tears sprung from my eyes at his blatant viewing, my hands slowed down to a slow caress as I struggled to stop the sobs of humiliation.

I blew out slowly, refusing to look at him, refusing to feed his sick desire. Blood roared through my veins, every fibre of my body repulsed, and nausea constricted my throat.

His lips twitched and a cruel, satisfied smile covered his face. "Rinse."

I snapped from my thoughts and picked up the shower head, shuddering when the stream of water flowed over my breasts, my nipples hardening with the sensation. It was nothing to do with sexual stimulant but for Daniel it obviously was as I caught his slight shift in the chair, his eyes hard as he scanned my body hungrily. Vomit filled my mouth but my heavy weeping kept it at bay as my throat closed in with the pressure of my cries. He continued to watch me, his eyes narrow. "Turn it off."

He picked up a fluffy white towel from the shelving unit and held it open. I stared at him as I reached out for it and he shook his head. "Come here."

I cautiously stepped into it and gulped when he wrapped it around me, completely encasing me inside the comforting softness. A gasp echoed from my chest as he scooped me up and held me in his arms, his embrace soothing and protective as he carried me across the hallway and into a bedroom. The conflicting emotions were torturous. I wanted to recoil from him, get as far away as possible from his hold, yet loneliness provided me with a deep want for comfort. I had to physically refrain from curling into him to seek solace, not just from him, from anyone, even though my body and mind were in need of a natural source of consolation.

The lavish décor in the bedroom took my breath. Huge heavy curtains draped the window, delicate floral paper covered the walls, and exquisite white iron furniture decorated the room.

He placed me gently on the bed and pulled up the thick, heavy duvet, tucking it under my chin. His fingers stroked over my head before his lips rested against my forehead. "Sleep, lamb."

I stared at him in amazement as he left the room and pulled the door closed gently behind him.

What – the – fuckety – fuck?

I continued to gape at the door, but as though he had cast a spell on me, my eyes drooped and I once again obeyed his orders and slept.

Chapter Five

I woke suddenly in the night, darkness surrounding me as furious shouts filled the air, each muffled yell jolting me more and more awake. I couldn't distinguish the words apart from *whore* and *useless* every now and again with a few *nows* thrown into the mix.

I slid my feet out of bed, my toes curling appreciatively into the deep pile as I padded across the room and pressed my ear to the door. I squinted as though that would aid my hearing. Why did people do that?

A female screamed and I shot backwards, my arse hitting the floor with a thud. I scrambled in reverse, climbing back into bed and pulling the duvet up around my neck just as the door opened and light flooded my eyes behind my eyelids.

I frantically tried to calm my breathing, trying to ease the storm banging at my breastbone as fear caused me to shudder even beneath the heat of the duvet.

The silence was thick and heavy, apprehension and anticipation clogging my throat as dread diluted my blood.

"Have you forgotten something, lamb?"

I clenched my teeth when he spoke, his voice was deep but steady, angry but calm and I knew deep within myself that anyone that controlled was very, *very* dangerous.

I peeked out from behind the bedding, my nose still under cover as my eyes focused on his dark silhouette, the outline of his muscled physique from the hallway light quite impressive.

"Well?"

I shuffled upright and stared at him as confusion rendered me candid and unreserved. "Eh?"

His brows shifted into his hairline and I tensed when his teeth sank into his lip, reminding me of his demand for obedience. "Oh, yes. I'm sorry."

I slid from the bed, shivering against the cold that rippled over my nakedness as I dropped to my knees by the bed. I scuffled into position, my backside on my heels, knees apart, chin up and hands on my thighs.

His black socks drew my attention as he paced the room towards me, the faint thump of his feet on the carpet giving my eyes something to focus on. "Good, but next time you'll remember without the need to be prompted."

Was he ever satisfied? I'd dropped to the floor as soon as I had remembered, what more did he want? In fact...

What the hell was I doing? Apart from prolonging my death by conceding to his demands. I wasn't his toy, his puppet or even his God damn slave. How dare he? How stupid was I? I'd woken up in a dismal damp room, chained up and left to starve and dehydrate and he expected me to fall at his feet, obey his every whim. The man who stood before me ruined my life, took from me what my mother had so painstakingly created. He'd taken my confidence, my self-respect, my thoughts, and my body and had morphed them into a living nightmare. He had constructed a corpse from a fun-loving girl.

He didn't deserve my surrender or my body and he would never own my mind, that was something I was sure of. That, out of everything moulded by anyone was mine, developed and nurtured by me, reared by me.

I shot to my feet suddenly, glaring at him, and he stepped back in surprise. "How dare you, you fucking freak! Who the fuck do you think you are? Hmm? You... you do whatever you do and you think I'm gonna follow every fucking order you spit at me? Well I have news for you!"

I took a step towards him, my eyes fixed on his neutral expression as my anger rose, the strong girl inside me fighting back, refusing to concede to the monster who fed from my fear. "I'm not your slave. I'm not a fucking object, I'm a person. I'm a woman with feelings, a girl with a heart and soul. I'm not yours. I'm not your possession. My mother birthed me, not you. You are nothing to me. You think because you took something from me once that I'll... I'll... what? That I'll just drop to my knees before you. Are you God? No, you are not! So stop fucking acting like it and take me home."

My chest heaved as he continued to stare at me. The silence was nauseating and I swallowed the fear that curled up my throat with his casual demeanour.

But fuck him and his demands. If he killed me right there, then so be it. I was born to fight, raised to persevere, and right then I was adamant I was holding the fuck on as hard as I could.

Two minutes passed before his head inclined to the side marginally and I saw his nostrils flare gently.

I stepped back when he took a step towards me. My mouth dried instantly as the sheer power he radiated engulfed me. He seemed to grow before me, his frame hardening as ice formed in his eyes. His shoulders tightened and his teeth sank into his lower lip.

I gulped as his tongue dipped out and trailed slowly across his bottom lip. "You seem to forget what I told you three years ago, Mae."

I hadn't been expecting that. What had he told me? I remembered every single word he had spat at me, it was engrained into my mind, never allowing me to forget and move on.

I frantically searched my memory, diving deep into the memories of that night, my mind replaying his words until I froze at the one I knew he meant.

"I am the sort of man who will relish in your defiance, Mae. Believe me; I would love nothing more than to fight you, to take you hard and punishingly, to bruise you and make you bleed."

And he had made me bleed, not just bodily but from my heart and soul. For three long years I hadn't stopped bleeding inside.

His lips curled when he knew I'd found the right memory, his smile sinister and mocking as his eyes glinted sharply. "You like to fight, little lamb?" he whispered as he took another step forward. "Or do you like to be punished?"

My legs trembled as my eyes searched the room for anything I could use as a weapon but my sights set on the door, the only means of escape. It was pointless, an impossible task that wasted valuable energy. His fist grabbed my hair as I shot past him, stopping me instantly. I fell to my knees by his side. "Oh, come on, Mae. You obviously enjoy the fight. Where's that spirit gone, huh?"

I screamed as he flung me across the room as though I weighed nothing, as though my body was filled with air. I hit the wall, pain exploding through every bone in my slight frame. I scrambled around, my legs giving way each time I tried to get to my feet, and every time I found my footing, he knocked me back down with a heavy fist.

It's astonishing what the human body can endure. I was so pumped on adrenaline that I didn't register the pain, I didn't feel the crack of each bone or the blood as it started to trickle from my beaten body. All I felt was survival, a deep-seated need to escape from him, nature's ability of making sure we didn't go down without a fight.

This continued for over twenty minutes, him waiting until I tried to right myself before he would take great pleasure in slamming me back down. I knew it was a game to him; I was his entertainment, a pawn there for his amusement.

I gave in and huddled against the corner of the room, my knees bent in front of me as I sobbed and the pain rendered me still.

He tutted and gave me a sad look. "Oh, don't give up, lamb. We haven't dealt with your filthy mouth yet. The fun has just started."

"You're a monster," I hissed at him, the final ember of anger reaching out defiantly. My spirit fought back, refusing to back down even though he and I already knew he had won.

A small smile twisted his lips, forming his already handsome face into something quite beautiful. But sometimes beauty masked ugliness, hid the deep hideousness that every single one of us possessed.

He stalked towards me almost gracefully, his long legs consuming the space between us quickly. He dropped to his haunches before me, causing me to shift backwards, to mould myself into the wall as he rested his forearms on his knees and regarded me.

"You seem to struggle to grasp the concept of this." He slid his tongue along his bottom lip and sighed as if saddened by my refusal to succumb to him. "Let me make this easy for you. I am a tutor and you, Mae, you are my apprentice. You will learn discipline, elegance, surrender. I will teach you to give everything that is required of you, and furthermore, you will learn to give willingly."

I swallowed and reared back further when he reached out and brushed away the hair that was stuck to the congealing blood on my mouth. "You will want to bestow pleasure, you will readily present your body to me and ultimately, you will voluntarily give me your soul."

"I will never give myself to you," I stuttered, hanging onto my resolve, albeit stupidly. "You will never own me."

He smirked and chuckled. "I don't think I explained myself accurately."

I whimpered when he grasped my jaw tightly, the spread of his fingers across my face painful and cruel. He yanked my chin upwards until my eyes met his angry glare, hatred and repulsion heavy in his eyes. "You are the lamb. I am the shepherd. I *will* control your every move. I *will* direct and govern you until you learn your place. And I *will* guide you along the path to your slaughter."

My stomach heaved at the sincerity in his voice, his ruthless promise that he would destroy me sending my heart into panic. "If that's what you want then why not kill me now?" I spat out. "Why teach me when the end goal for you is to see me stripped, hung and quartered like a piece of meat in a butcher's window? Why drag this out?"

His eyes twinkled as we had already slipped into the teacher and pupil role with my query. He bit into the tip of his tongue and smirked. "Do you know nothing about a hunter and his prey? Why a predator stretches out the hunt?"

He paused as if actually waiting for me to answer. I remained quiet, staring at him in disgust. He pursed his lips, pulled in a breath then smiled softly. "It's all part of the fun, lamb. The entertainment and thrill is beyond exciting. It's a stimulant, a drug almost. And let's face it, we all enjoy the odd high now and again."

He continued to watch me, waiting for me to answer and just as victory crossed his face I fixed my stare on him, knowing I was defying him with that simple action. "You will never pen me in like some timid animal that is too scared to fight. I have nothing to lose. You can beat me, hurt me, control me even, but you will never ever own me." And I would make sure he never did. I was born Mae Swift, my parent's little tower of strength. I needed to not only prove to them that I was strong, but also to myself. My parents' legacy would fight all the damn way... right up to the end if need be.

A flicker of fury ghosted his eyes before he regained his composure and laughed with a mocking quality. "We'll see, Mae. But I can promise that I will enjoy the hunt. I will most definitely relish in your destruction. When you yield and give yourself over to me it will be as luxurious as witnessing your despair along the way."

I forced myself to hold his stare, refusing his need for dominance.

Our contract had just been signed but my fate had been decided before his words had even left his mouth. However, he underestimated just how little I had to give. His game wouldn't even see the players reach the end square; he would never relish in the victory of the end game. My life was a game of snakes and ladders; my route through life had always presented snakes at every roll of the dice, constant downward spirals no matter how hard I had fought to reach a ladder.

And it was this knowledge that helped me challenge him at every square on the board.

Chapter Six

'"Lessons lead us into knowledge.'

I shivered against the gentleness of his touch, the tips of his fingers tracing each ridge of my spine from the dip in my lower back up to the nape of my neck.

"Such beauty," he whispered as his fingers bunched my hair aside, placing it across my shoulder and granting him full exposure to my neck.

His lips settled almost teasingly on the edge of my hairline as his fingers ventured onwards, up the length of my arms until each of his hands encompassed the cuffs around my wrists.

He'd softly woken me as soon as the birds had started their morning serenade, placing a gentle kiss to my cheek. I'd scurried back, much to his displeasure. The fire that had morphed his handsome face at my defiance had been chilling and disturbing. The storm in his eyes had provoked me into action, reminding me that I now belonged to him, no one else, not even myself, only him.

He would never understand that I was now willing to give myself to him though. I'd fought him at first, right to the very edge of my sanity. But alone in the darkness with only hatred and despair to keep me company in the previous two days of solitary, punishment for my outburst, I had recognised some astonishing facts about myself.

What did I have worth fighting for? The end was close; too close now. There was no one who would be there for me, no one who would hold my hand as the angels heralded my arrival. No one who would mourn the end of my existence, not a single person, apart from maybe Spud would watch me join the many others in the field of graves.

Maybe Daniel would grant a swifter passing, stop the debilitation of my illness and offer the end to my anguish. I was ready for death, maybe even hungry for it. Peace and extinction were welcoming; the finality of them comforting and euphoric.

"Why spoil such perfection, lamb? The marks you decorate yourself with are nothing but masks hiding the real you that begs to be seen."

I didn't answer, I wasn't expected to. It was the first day of my 'education' he'd told me as I'd scrambled to my knees before him in the bedroom. He'd led me to the 'correction centre' as I so aptly named it; the room I had begun this adventure in. The room with the cross, the room with the chains, the room with the many instruments lined up orderly along a wall. The dark, damp chamber that fed the sinister in my Master and nourished his need for control and order.

"Do you relish in the pain of your torture, Mae?" he continued, giving me permission to answer him with the use of my name.

"Yes, Master."

I had learnt quickly, his furious belts across my cheek had encouraged it. His venomous words of instruction had engrained his conditions swiftly into me. He'd made me recite the alphabet time after time, and every single letter had to be accompanied by 'Master' – 'A, Master. B, Master. C, Master….' And so on. Each time I slipped and forgot, his palm connected with my cheek. Although I was grateful it hadn't been his fist, it was still something that had quickly soaked into my mind until it became second nature to answer him with 'Master'.

I hated myself for surrendering to his wants, but pain had caused my instinct to defend myself to kick in. And if calling him Master halted that pain, then so be it. I was all for easy right then, and although fight still flowed amidst my blood, my mind had found the easiest route possible through this nightmare.

"Tell me how it makes you feel when you cut."

His demand triggered an involuntary tremble through my blood, firing up my internal need for release and calm. I swallowed hesitantly, wondering how to word the unique sensation that empowered me each time the blood spilled from my veins.

"Do not hesitate at my questioning, Mae." He tugged on my hair, whipping my head backwards painfully until his face was upside down in my vision. The hold on my wrists from the chains provided a sharp pull with his blunt movement. "Truth comes with urgency. Indecision brings on lies."

"It…" I gulped and blew out a slow breath. "It helps me heal, Master."

He was silent, his eyes narrow but clear as he traced them over my face. His expression held both understanding as well as curiosity. He nodded in reply as he released his harsh hold on my hair.

I startled when his breath heated my cheek, his mouth against my ear. "Do you need release, lamb? Are you begging for the comfort of pain?" He seemed almost pleased with me, happy that I welcomed pain and suffering. I assumed this made my training easier, my spirit already spoilt and eager for discipline.

"Yes, Master." I answered him as quickly as possible as a trickle of hope spread through me, excitement kindling my need for stimulation.

His hand slid down my back, his palm sweeping softly over my buttocks. I gasped when he glided further, the whole of his hand now pressing over my sex. This was the first time he had touched me sexually. I was surprised at this. The first time, three years ago, it had been his main mission to take my innocence as brutally as possible. Yet now there seemed some ulterior motive for my imprisonment.

"Punishment seems to be reward for you, Mae. I'm not sure how to give when you have nothing to offer in exchange."

A sliver of anger heated my belly at his false temptation. It was obvious he never gave anything willingly, always wanting something in return.

His nose buried into the dip of skin behind my ear as he pushed the heel of his hand onto my clitoris, igniting a surge of desire through me. The feeling was new. I never felt desire; the human impulse to procreate had been taken away from me when my innocence was ripped away so cruelly.

The strange sensation of lust caused the air in my lungs to still. Master's scent assaulted my nostrils, the pure sex he radiated amplified my desire. Disgust and self-hatred rolled over me. He was doing it again, manipulating my emotions with his touch and attention, making the need to please mix with the abhorrence of revulsion.

He suddenly pulled back and I let out the breath I had been holding. I ignored the throb that my body was pulsing wildly with, disgusted with nature's carnality as he strolled across the room.

I tracked his finger as he ran it slowly over each of the tools he had ready for my 'punishment'. "Which appeals to you, Mae?"

His offer confused me but I answered quickly, as was expected of me. "The blade, Master."

He cocked his head to the side without turning to look at me. I could sense his shock. He'd expected me to pick something easy and light, yet those items did nothing for me.

He guided his hand to the small scalpel that rested against a larger knife and paused. "This one?"

"Yes, Master." My voice was small and wheezy as enthusiasm turned the air in my lungs to vapour, excitement humming headily through my bloodstream.

"Is this what you used on your face, lamb? The tool that marred your beauty?"

I did stall then. How did he know? It had been over two years since the incident. Did he know the rest of the story regarding the day I defaced myself?

He turned on his heels and narrowed his eyes, his chest heaving against the crisp white shirt he wore. His physique was lean and hard, his sculptured muscles straining the material as his rage pulled it taut. "Answer me!"

I narrowed my own eyes, still mystified how he knew I had abused myself. Anyone else would have presumed that an attack of some sorts was the reason for the scar that ran straight through the right side of my face, *especially* as it was to my face.

He threw down the blade angrily, the clang of the metal on the concrete jolting me in surprise. My eyes widened when he picked up a riding crop, the long, thin instrument his own obvious choice now punishment was called for.

I squeezed my eyes shut when he brought it down swiftly on my backside, fire spreading across my skin and taking my breath. I was too shocked to scream. The pain I always punished myself with was nowhere near this devastating, a fraction of this agony now scorching over my ass.

"Shit!" I hissed as he lashed another strike over the already delicate skin.

The chains above my head rattled vigorously when he knocked me sideways with a fist to my face. "There's that filthy mouth again, lamb." His anger was unbridled as he appeared before me, spit flying onto my face.

"FUCK YOU!" I roared, spontaneous anger over-ruling the pain pulsing my cheek, bringing out my insolence and need to challenge his discipline.

He shook his head angrily, his face morphing before me as the whole of his hand covered my nose and mouth, restricting both my available inputs of air.

I yanked against him as his other hand wrapped into my long hair, twisting until I couldn't move my head. "You disgusting cunt. The filth you spew disturbs me."

I was gasping for breath, my lungs squealing in panic when the remaining pockets of oxygen keeping me alive depleted rapidly. My brain throbbed against my skull as starvation tortured it.

I tried to shake my head at him, my eyes watering and bulging as his own angry slits watched the life drain from me. My chest stuttered as a pain tore through my breastbone with the pressure in my lungs.

I endeavoured to apologise with my eyes, begging him to stop as my vision tunnelled and my body sagged against the restraints.

He released his hold as suddenly as he had brought it on, leaving me panting and wheezing, my lungs burning with the sudden fuel inflating them.

"Will you ever learn, Mae? Will you ever heed my advice? That smut you speak repulses men, therefore lowering your value."

I snapped my eyes to his and stared at him, my chest struggling to cope with the oxygen and shock. "What did you say?"

He scoffed and shook his head, a cruel sneer curling his lip. "What? You thought *I* wanted you? That *I* desire you?"

His words shouldn't have hurt me as much as they did and I looked away, blinking back the pain that settled in my gut at his ridicule and rejection. What the hell was wrong with me?

"Did you think I was forming you into something that I would want?" he continued as he stepped closer to me. He laughed mockingly as his disgusted gaze roamed my body. "You are nothing but a whore. I prefer my conquests to be clean and pure."

My mouth dropped open as anger surged through me. "I would be innocent if you hadn't forced it from me, you bastard!"

He crashed into me, his fist once more bruising my lip as his fingers wrestled with the cuffs on my wrists. I dropped to the floor as soon as they snapped open but I didn't have chance to feel the impact before I was being dragged across the concrete by my hair. Instinct brought my hand up to curl my fingers around his grip but it was an impossible task, his grasp was too tight.

He threw me onto the floor, his wrath sucking the air from the room. I drew back, scuttling into the wall when he started to unbuckle his belt. My eyes shot up to his, angering him further when he yanked his zip down and pulled out his cock. I quickly diverted my gaze. Although twenty-one, it was actually the first time I'd set eyes on one. My cheeks flooded with heat as he barked out a cruel laugh.

"Oh come on, lamb. You asked for it."

I shook my head at him, denying his words. "No…"

"Oh, but you did. Your expression told me everything when I told you I didn't desire you. My declaration ached your heart, I saw it."

I shook my head again as he stepped to me and grabbed my hair, pulling me to my knees before him with my face to his groin. I winced as he dug his fingers into my jaw and forced my mouth open. "You use your teeth, then I will delight in pulling each and every one from your mouth."

I knew he meant every word; torture fed his dark side, fuelled his black heart.

I choked on the tears when he pushed his length into my mouth. A shudder ripped through him as his grip on my hair started to control my movement, directing his own pleasure. I sank my lips around him, the act natural and instinctive. He hissed faintly and my eyes lifted to his. His jaw was tight, his teeth clenched together as he drew air through his nose noisily, his strong chest rising and falling rapidly.

I whimpered as his expression changed from anger to awe, as though surprised by my ability to suck on him. It was hardly rocket science; however, even I was shocked by my reflexive worship. His whole face softened and his eyes widened. He released my hair with one hand and drew his thumb across my cheek, wiping away a tear that had slid free.

"That's it," he urged softly as he pulled and pushed gentler, his rhythm slow as I pleasured him with my mouth.

I was amazed at the taste and texture. I had expected repulsion as my tongue tickled the underside of him, but I was shocked to find I didn't mind the unique taste.

He grew hungrier, his hips pumping faster as he started to groan. Fire filled my belly as my pussy pulsed heavily. I was turned on by something sickening, something cruel and twisted. Shame surged through me but Master smiled as he slipped his thumb into the corner of my mouth alongside his cock.

The pressure between my thighs grew with the simple action. His moans intensified and I released one of my own, vibrating the tremor around his cock. He hissed violently and swelled further inside my mouth. My nipples hardened as I saw the rapture on his face explode when his cock did inside my mouth. I savoured it, hungrily devouring every drop.

I had watched him succumb to my deliverance. I had given him a weakness, a pleasure he hadn't expected. And although sickening, it energised me, gave me a sliver of influence over him. I had witnessed his knees buckle, his heartbeat pound in the base of his neck and his breathing stutter from something I had done, a moment of role reversal, and damn, if I didn't feel euphoric.

He stepped back, put his cock back in his trousers and walked away. I stared at the door when it closed behind him, blinking at his indifference to me.

I had been wrong. What I thought had been a glimpse at his weakness had actually been my own. I had been stupid enough to think I was different from any other woman who had sucked on his cock. I had foolishly thought I had been the only one to ever pleasure him, whereas the reality was, to him I was just another whore, another woman who gave him pleasure.

My stomach revolted at the twist in my mind, the humiliation of what I had enjoyed when I should have felt nothing but disgust.

I flung my body round and vomited into the corner of the room, gagging at the taste when realisation of what I was throwing up hit me. I crawled across the floor to get away from it.

Abhorrence found me at the same time I found the scalpel Master had slung away so easily.

Chapter Seven

'Take the burden, never give it to
others.'

His face was a haze, almost eerie as he stormed
towards me. I tipped my head slowly, my movements
stunted but composed.

He really was quite stunning; the power of him
both physical and psychological. His body gave
reason to idolise him; strong, lean and hard. The
rawness to him, the perfection of his physique
demanded attention whilst the supremacy he
radiated ordered obedience and submission.

His anger was palpable, suffocating as he neared
me. Yet in my calm I smiled up at him. He crouched
before me, his face almost glowing in fury.

He ripped my arms from my sides and tore his
eyes over the deep red lines decorating my pale skin.
The pattern of blood trailing down my arms
resembled tiny rivulets journeying to the ocean,
begging for escape. They really were quite orderly;
four scarlet lines of my life, each trail straggling down
the centre of each of my four fingers until deep ruby
teardrops wept from the tips of my fingers.

He pulled out a phone from his pocket and stabbed
at the keys angrily. "I need you in the school. Bring
Frank," was all he said before he terminated the call
and shoved the phone back in the inside pocket of his
suit jacket.

I smiled at his tie, the deep red colour an exact replica of my arms. Reaching out slowly, I ran my finger down the length of it. Master never flinched as his eyes followed my daring move, the deepness to his gaze soft and troubled as he let out a deep sigh.

"This is very nice," I whispered.

I jolted when his palm softly settled on my cheek and his eyes found mine. "Why do this, Mae?"

He used my name, therefore ordering an answer from me. "It feels so good."

He parted his lips as he ran his thumb over my cheekbone. "It is no longer your job to do this. It is now my privilege, lamb. Your pain belongs to me, your need for release is now mine to provide." He held my gaze when I sighed contentedly. "Do you understand, Mae?"

"Yes," I breathed as my body still tingled under the intoxication controlling my mind. His words were comforting, physically embracing me under his concern. He cared for me. He wanted to help me in my need for oblivion; he intended to be the one to bring me relief. "You want to please me, love me," I spoke candidly.

He reared back as though shocked by my statement. His eyes darkened. I shivered as his care morphed into cruelty. "Oh, lamb, you misinterpret again."

I swallowed nervously when he pressed his thumb deeply into one of the slices still pulsing with my blood. An ache of need throbbed in my belly when he then slid his thumb down the trail, following the path of my wreckage. He leaned further into me until his mouth hovered against my ear, his hot breath tickling the few wisps of hair against my neck. "Your blood is mine, Mae. It is your life force, the very thing that feeds you. But now I substitute your blood. *I* am your life force, the very thing that will feed you, whether it be pain, misery or fucking pleasure. *I* am what will breathe life into you, not the air; *me*. *I* will be the one that controls each and every move you make, not your brain; *me*. *I* am now the very thing that will decide if you live or die, not your blood; *me*."

His statement squeezed my heart painfully, choking me in the truth of his words. I should have known he wouldn't care about me; no one did, so why start now?

I laughed and nodded. "Of course, Master. I apologise. How utterly stupid of me to think that a single entity on this fucking..."

I hissed as his fist once again connected with my lip, more blood spraying furiously from my body. I was surprised I had any left to feed my brain.

"Will you control your mouth!"

I nodded and lowered my eyes as a faint knock echoed in the room and the door opened. A young, slim woman entered the room. Her thick blonde mane was pulled into a pony tail behind her head, the skin on her face taut with the extreme pull of it. Her sharp blue eyes narrowed on me as her bright red lips pursed. Her large chest heaved under the strain of the cream silk shirt she wore, her hips fairly wide under the tightness of her knee length skirt.

Her lips curled at the edge as she sneered at me. "Oh dear." Her tone was mocking and amused, her disgust at my appearance pleasing her very much.

I shifted my eyes from her to Master then back again, immediately recognising what they were. Lovers. She reeked of sex and need, her eyes softening instantly when they landed on Master. "I'll fix her up. You need to leave for your meeting."

Master nodded as he stood, his eyes never leaving mine. "Make sure she's secured after, Demi. I'll deal with her later." He was speaking to Demi but his eyes remained fixed on mine. I frowned at the slither of something that passed through them, it was soft but heated, gentle but debauched and I gulped at the sudden intensity he studied me with.

He turned sharply to face the large man who had entered behind Demi. "I need the equipment securing."

The man I presumed to be Frank nodded once, acknowledging the order. He never opened his mouth to speak and he never looked at me once.

Master turned to me, the previous expression gone and replaced with a deep-seated hatred. "Let Demi do her job without interference or disgust."

I stared at him as my brow furrowed. What the fuck did he mean 'without disgust'?

"Answer me, Mae!"

"Yes, Master," I mumbled.

He narrowed his eyes further before he turned to Demi. "Behave." She gave a simple nod at the order and a small smile as she watched him leave.

She strolled over to me when the door slid closed behind Master, the clip of her heels on the cement floor loud and hypnotising. I looked up at her from my position against the wall, my arse numb with the hardness under it.

She tutted and sighed at me. "You really are quite something." I wasn't sure if it was a compliment or sarcasm. She dropped to her knees and I soon found out it was the latter. "You filthy tramp. Look at you. Your need for attention repulses me."

"D...Demi!" Frank stuttered a warning from across the room.

We both turned to him. He was looking at us but his eyes were hard and blank. His body was huge, the width of him as considerable as his height. His eyes were cold and empty but his face appeared soft and almost childlike. His short blonde hair was cut to perfection, almost military in form. Both of his large bulky arms were adorned with a mass of ink, large faces of ladies and numerous weapons decorating his skin in various colours. I wasn't sure what it was about him that soothed me but he exuded a tangible serenity, even with the sheer size of him.

"Go to hell, F...Frank," Demi mocked with a hiss of hatred to her voice. Her jeer at Frank's speech impediment made my blood boil.

She pulled out some things from a small box and I watched, mesmerised as she threaded a needle with suturing thread. "You obviously enjoy pain, rat, so I'll not bother anaesthetising your arm."

Frank sighed heavily and I lifted my focus to him as Demi started her torturous procedure. Every harsh stab of the needle made me wince but I sank my teeth into my lip, refusing to let her witness my discomfort. She was obviously a bitch, a heartless cow who thought she remained above the rankings of others. Her idolisation of Master was just as apparent as her hatred for me.

I smiled at Frank when his eyes kept flicking in my direction. He never smiled back and his gaze never roamed over my bare body but his eyes softened with each of my attempts to connect with him. He seemed the lesser of the two evils in the room and I desperately tried to relate to him with each of my looks.

I winced when Demi speared my skin deeper than was necessary. I dropped my eyes to study her suturing. My eyes widened at the hacked attempt at repair. The stitches were large and angry and would most definitely leave more of a scar than my track lines would have.

Frank shook his head in anger as he checked out Demi's work. "F...Fuck sake, Demi. D...Daniel told you to fix her up, not m...mar the poor girl."

Demi shot upright and glared in his direction. "One, never call Master Daniel in front of the stock, you retard. Two, never question my motives, and three, keep your senseless opinions to yourself. Master won't tolerate your contempt towards me."

He stared at her, his eyes cooling further with every passing moment. His hands fisted by his sides as his throat bobbed with his fury. Eventually, he relented under Demi's glare and shook his head.

I flinched when Demi's fingers wrapped around my hair and she pulled me across the room. "Get the fuck off me, you bitch," I spat as I attempted to yank her fingers from their cruel hold.

I choked on the blood when she rammed one of her heels into the side of my face, the tip dislodging a tooth under the force of it. Coughing loudly, I spat the tooth out with a mouthful of blood.

Her eyes widened as anguish covered her face. My hand lifted instinctively to my cheek, holding my face as the pain throbbed. "Ahh, shit," I mumbled.

Demi pointed one of her long talons at Frank, her eyes blazing in severity. "She fell into the wall."

Frank lowered his eyes, worry evident on his face. His eyes moved over my face, softening when they landed on the trail of blood trickling from the corner of mouth. "B...But..."

"No buts, freak. I'm warning you." She turned to me. "If either of you tell Master then I will make your lives miserable. There are so many things I can tell him that you did today, like how you punched me, how your language was pure filth and how evil you were to me."

My eyes widened. "What? I haven't even..." The funny sensation of talking with a gap in my teeth made my brow furrow even further.

"No," she butted in. "But Master isn't aware of that, is he? And if you think he'll believe you, rat, over me then I'm afraid you're in for a shock." She bent into me, her face a mere inch from mine, her hatred almost slapping me. "*MY* Master loves me and he will give me anything I ask. And if I ask him to slice straight through your heart, he won't even hesitate."

She gripped my chin, rendering more pain through the delicate nerves in my gum. "You not only belong to Master Daniel, but also to me. I am free to do whatever I wish and I'm hoping you understand just how low I will go to please *MY* Master."

I chewed on the inside of my cheek, trying to hide my humour at her desperation. "Honey," I whispered, "You are more than welcome to him, but why do I get the feeling you feel threatened by me?"

I glowed inwardly as she squirmed slightly, her teeth becoming visible when they sank into her bottom lip.

I smirked when I realised how deep her need for Master was. And me being me didn't hesitate in twisting that knife even deeper. "Oh, I think you ought to feel threatened. I made him come in my mouth almost as soon as he sank his cock between my lips."

Frank mumbled a groan as Demi transformed before me. Her eyes fired and her fingers dug even further into my cheeks, her thumb pressing hard against the empty area between my back molars. "He touched you?" Her surprise was potent, the shock of my revelation burning her blood.

"Well," I sneered. "Rather, I touched him. Just a little something to please *your* Master. Blew his load straight down my throat whilst he cried out my name."

Okay, maybe that was a little stretched, but I wasn't going to tell her that he never uttered my name, and disappeared before I could even swallow the whole mouthful he'd given me. There was just something about this bitch that got my back up, brought out the dark side of me, the side that was adamant I would knock her down after her ridicule over Frank's disability.

"You lying whore," she spat as her fist crashed into my face.

Fuck that!

I gave it back to her, her face crumpling under my fists. She was easy prey in my desperation to release the pent up energy. She just lay still as her ugly fucking face smashed to pieces under my wrath while I let my hatred out and tore into her. Adrenaline fired through me, killing any pain in my arm and allowing me to strike blow after blow upon the bitch.

I knew Master would kill me, but bring it on. The quicker the better. I couldn't take another moment in there, tied, beaten and regarded lower than a dog. Maybe this would bring the finality that awaited me in the next few months hurtling forward, ending my anguish over how my life would end, how painful it would be when my soul ripped its way out of me.

"N...No..." Frank begged as he pulled me off the bitch who was curled up below me. I kicked out at her as my body was hauled backwards. "You m...mustn't. Master will p...punish you, Mae."

"I don't care!" I screamed as I struggled to free myself from his hold and kill the contemptuous bitch whimpering in a heap on the floor.

I bucked against Frank when he forced my wrists into the cuffs hanging from the ceiling. "I…I apolog…gise but I m…must secure y…you."

Demi uncurled herself and clambered up, her eyes fierce on me. "You cunt!"

I laughed. "Oooh don't let Daniel hear the filth you spew," I mocked, my mind completely overtaken with my delirium. "He won't like that, Demi."

She huffed and wiped the blood from her mouth with the back of her hand, her eyes studying the red substance that now smeared her smooth, flawless skin. She looked shocked to discover she actually housed a blood system, her eyes staring widely as her lips parted. That figured.

She strolled over to the tools on the wall, her shoulders straight in her determination to hurt me. Her long fingers rested on a large iron baton. My breath hitched and I tested the security of my restraints. It didn't surprise me to find they were not only steady but strict and harsh, denying me any movement at all.

"Get out," she ordered Frank.

He shook his head frantically as his eyes swept from me to Demi, who brandished the stick she was going to teach me a lesson with. "M…Master won't t…tolerate this, D…Demi."

Demi scoffed and smiled arrogantly. "I'm sure he'll forgive me. After all, the rancid rat hurt his baby."

I closed my eyes and sighed. The bitch had planned it all along. I realised as Frank quietly lowered his face and walked from the room that I had played right into her hands. I was a fool. I always had been. Even after everything, I still held onto the hope that one day someone somewhere would actually like me, love me even. And yet, even though my life was nearly over, my hopes were always buried under the taunt of hopelessness.

Demi pulled in a large breath and smiled at me, her eyes glistening in delight as she raised the baton above her head. "Let's get to know one another a little better, rat."

I closed down after she rained carnage, the pain in my body too intense with her malicious hits. She didn't just beat me; she battered and crushed me in her explosion of fury. She screamed with every strike, blanketing my own cries as the agony rendered me almost numb.

Oblivion took my mind to a better place after she moved behind me and crashed the stick into the back of my knees, jolting my wrists and snapping my joints at the pressure.

However, I didn't lose consciousness until I heard Frank re-enter and force Demi's wrath upon himself. Each of his cries scorched my heart as he took the punishment for me.

Chapter Eight

'The hunt for love preys on the soul.'

The sear that ran through my skull was crippling, its intensity debilitating. Panic surged through me as sickness threatened to choke me. It had never been this bad, the torment this time was excruciating.

I moaned as I turned my face to the side, my body refusing any movement, then released the explosive illness clogging my throat, vomit trickling down my cheek.

I heard soft footfalls on carpet but my eyes refused to open, not daring to risk more torture.

I murmured a groan when a cool cloth swept over my mouth, gently collecting the remnants of my illness as delicate fingers brushed the hair from my face, perspiration gluing it to my hot skin.

"Sshhh."

"Mmm." I couldn't speak any more thanks and hoped my nurse understood my gratitude.

"Sleep, lamb."

I stiffened, the simple action tearing explosions through my brain. I blew out a harsh breath at the throb when I struggled to open my eyes. My heavy eyelids squealed furiously as I battled with their stubborn refusal to cede to my demand.

Master's face slowly came into focus as he perched beside me on the bed. He was minus his customary suit jacket, just a crisp, light blue shirt covering his impressive torso. The sleeves were rolled up to his elbows and the top two buttons were open, giving me a glimpse of fine dark hair.

"Sleep, Mae," he repeated more sternly.

I stared at him, however my gaze was soft as I relayed my message of thanks to his tendering. He replied in understanding with a faint nod, his dark chocolate eyes melting into me. He was the most handsome man I had ever bore witness to in my short twenty one years. If he was a nice person he would have been truly magnificent, many women I estimated, fighting for his attention. But his cruel personality masked the beauty, made it irrelevant.

Another surge of fire shot across the crown of my head and I instinctively brought my hands up to my head to cradle the pain. My knees bent as I pulled my legs up to my chest to protect myself from the torture.

"Is it unbearable?" he asked in a soft voice.

"Mmm," I mumbled sharply as I squeezed my eyes closed. I gagged at the pain, concentrating on my breathing like I'd been shown at the pain clinic but it was useless this time. "Need – meds."

"I'm afraid I can't grant access to your own, Mae, but Dr Galloway will be here shortly."

"What?"

"Just try and sleep, Mae... please."

I gulped and reopened my eyes, fighting against the pain to look at him. Did he know? Was he aware of *it*? "Why have you called a doctor?" My voice was slurred but coherent.

His eyebrow lifted. "Do you really need to ask, Mae?"

"I need to…" I hissed and shuddered as a bolt of white hot pain shot through the front of my skull causing my lips to tremble at the agony.

"Mae," Master snapped harshly. "Close your eyes and refrain from any more talk. Your body is beaten too much, and your blood pressure is raised causing pressure on your brain which in turn is aggravating your Glioma."

I wheezed at his words, my heart stuttering as my brain struggled to cope with his knowledge. "You know?" I forced out, gritting my teeth as the movement of my jaw pounded my head.

He snapped upright, his fury now palpable in the quiet room. "I shall not ask again, lamb. Your disobedience is giving me cause to want to hurt you. We both know you are in no fit state to take any more right now. I will return when Dr Galloway arrives. Until then, I suggest you heed my wishes if you value your peace."

If I could have opened my eyes I would have glared at him, the arrogant fucker. *'I suggest you heed my wishes if you value your peace.'* Who the hell spoke like that? In fact as I thought more about him, the more complex his dialogue appeared. He was always longwinded in his speech instead of getting to the point like most of us. His words were complex and intelligent, his accent privileged and almost snooty.

I curled my lip in answer. What – the – fuck – ever! I couldn't be arsed with him.

My lip curled higher when I noticed the immense difference in our vocalisations, my mouth in the gutter and his wrapped in silver.

Ahh, fuck him. I was Mae Swift, and no one, not even a Master with a penchant for cruelty would ever change that.

It was light when I next woke. Voices filled the quiet and I left my eyelids in place, listening to the conversation.

"Are there no other drugs available?" Master asked. "Something of greater potency?"

A male sigh echoed around the room. "There are but they are expensive, Daniel."

"Give them to her."

A pause stilled the air. I could sense who I presumed to be Dr Galloway's shock. "To what limit?"

"There are no limits. Treat her tumour and her pain."

"If you're sure?" The doctor sighed.

"Don't question me, Philip. It is none of your concern. Your only role is to make her more comfortable."

I whimpered when something scratched at my upper arm. A deep sensation of utter calm and serenity took me into the blackness.

"Drink," a soft female voice ordered as soon as I opened my eyes. A middle-aged, portly woman smiled softly at me, lines appearing beside her eyes. "How are you feeling, love?"

My headache had eased to a dull throb, and my body ached but nothing compared to how much it had hurt before. "Sore."

Her eyes narrowed as she looked down over my body. I was surprised to find I was clothed, a long, soft pink nightdress covering my modesty. "Mmm." That was all she murmured as she helped me up to lean on the bedhead.

"How long have I... been out?"

She sighed as she poured water from a jug into a crystal glass. "Around two weeks on and off."

My eyes widened as I sipped at the water she held to my lips, greedily enjoying the luxury of the cool liquid soothing the burn in my throat.

"Are you hungry?"

I nodded. She replied with a smile as she lifted off the bed. "Soup?"

"Yes," I whispered, stunned at how things had rapidly changed. "Please."

Her smile grew with my manners, her wide, toothy grin motherly and comforting. "I'll be right back."

She closed the door behind her and I glanced around the room. This wasn't my room. It was softer, the colours muted and easier than where I had slept before. Huge rose coloured curtains hung from the window, the delicate floral pattern matching both the bed linen and the soft furnishings decorating the room.

I gasped when my gaze landed on a mural of sorts decorating the longest wall. Butterflies, thousands of them, flittered over the paintwork, a rainbow of colours and a pattern of wings instantly drawing me in.

I lowered my feet to the floor, grimacing at the dull pain through my beaten body as I pushed myself upright and shuffled across the room. My legs wobbled but I put it down to the seizure of unused muscles as I made my way to the wall.

It was stunning, each butterfly pressing out of the wall. They weren't real but the way they had been crafted was spellbinding, they looked and felt real as I stroked the tip of my finger across a particular pale blue one that called for my attention. The softness to its faux wings tickled my fingertip, making me smile faintly.

"Holly Blue."

I spun round, wincing at the pain that tore through my knees with the sudden action.

"Sorry?" I asked as Master stepped through the door, his eyes intent on me.

"The butterfly. It's called Holly Blue."

"Oh." He walked towards me while I turned back to the wall. "It's…" I paused and shivered as he came to rest beside me, his huge body shrouding me. "Beautiful."

"Yes." He sighed deeply. "It is. Delicate and simply stunning."

I nodded, the gentle blueness of it giving me reason to smile. "Do you like butterflies?" I asked as I kept my gaze on the flurry before me. "Are they your *thing*?"

He was silent and I turned to study him. A small smile curved the corners of his lips as a twinkle lit his eyes, transforming his usual stern features into something of pure beauty. "My *thing*?"

"Yeah," I shrugged. "You know; your hobby, the thing that floats your boat, your diversion... your *thing*."

He diverted his eyes as he tried to hide his amusement. "No, Mae. Butterflies are not my *thing*."

I nodded, wondering why the hell he had a whole wall decorated with fake butterflies if they didn't appeal to him. "So whose thing are they? I mean, you don't decorate a whole fifteen foot wall with the insects if they do nothing for you."

The air around me physically cooled, oxygen rapidly depleting from the atmosphere. I knew instantly I had asked the wrong question.

"Nadu, Mae," he ordered suddenly, causing me to jump in surprise.

"I'm sorry. I didn't mean to pry."

His teeth sank into his bottom lip, his customary habit alerting me to his fury. I dropped to my knees before him as quickly as I could manage, shifting into the required pose as I stared straight forward. My eyes widened when I noticed the strain in the crotch of his trousers. The arsehole was turned on. What the fuck?

My breath paused when he calmly strolled around behind me, the unknown frightening as anguish flooded my body. I gasped when his hand pressed on the back of my head and he pushed me downwards until my forehead rested on the carpet, my arse stuck up in the air behind me.

"Place your hands on the back of your neck, lamb."

"What?" I spluttered as I tried to turn to him.

He was suddenly framing me, his strong body pressing against my back as his hot breath rippled over my ear. "You will refrain from any questioning. I ask, you obey. Is that clear?" I squeezed my eyes closed as he once again pressed my forehead to the floor. "IS THAT CLEAR?"

"Yes, Master," I spat, trying to control my temper.

"Again!"

"Yes," I whimpered as he grabbed a handful of my hair and twisted it, my roots screaming in pain at his hold. "Yes, Master," I repeated as I quickly brought my hands to clasp behind my neck.

His grasp loosened immediately. "Open your thighs."

Nausea curled deep as my stomach revolted to his demand. Heat flooded my cheeks as I obeyed and shuffled my aching knees apart.

Mortification hit me when he lifted my nightdress and cool air caused goosebumps to erupt over my backside. I shivered as one of his fingers traced the groove between my buttocks, the tip of his finger pressing against my anus. "Please..." I begged but shuddered when he slid the very tip inside. I blew out a breath as heat travelled into my stomach, my thighs rippling with desire as I fought against the treacherous sensation.

He pushed in further, the sensation unfamiliar and shameful. "Please don't."

My breath paused in my lungs as a scurry of arousal ripped through me. *Oh Christ!* I should be revolted by his touch, horrified. However, his contact did none of those things. I whimpered with shame when my body took control and my hips pressed backwards, seeking more of his pleasure.

I started to pant when he slid his finger in and out slowly, the pleasure building until my body throbbed in need, my brain crying out for release as my blood swelled inside my veins. "Please," I repeated but this time with a completely different meaning.

"You see how I own you, lamb. How willing your body is to succumb to me."

I nodded; my throat had closed up to the sensations running through me. "Oh, God," I rasped when his stroke sped up. My backside burnt when he inserted another finger but when the initial pain subsided, all that remained was bliss and need, want and desire.

"Tell me what you want, Mae."

I gulped, embarrassment leading to shame. "I... I don't know... I just need..."

"You need me to make you come. You want me to provide you with the oblivion of climax." It was a statement, not a question and I nodded. Fuck yes, I did need him to make me come. It felt like my life depended on it, the pressure ready to blow my mind if it wasn't set free soon.

"Yes. Please.... Oh, God, please, Master."

My whole body went into lockdown as my first ever orgasm floored me. Every single muscle in my body tightened as his fingers pounded deeply and more fingers pinched my clit hard. A silent scream erupted from my throat as my back arched, the sore muscles screeching in pleasure at the pain.

I couldn't breathe, my lungs had constricted. A deep throb fired up my spine and pulsed bliss through my brain, dragging a deep sigh from me as my forehead dropped to the floor once more, but this time in need instead of demand.

"Oh fuck!" I breathed out as ecstasy rippled through me.

Oh fuck! I tensed as soon as it left my lips, hoping I'd said it quiet enough for Master to miss. Yep, no such luck.

I screamed as a fire struck my bottom, the palm of his hand cracking my flesh. "I'm sorry," I cried out as another blow stripped my poor skin.

He remained silent as he rained stroke after stroke on my tender skin, each crack firing painfully through me. Yet, when his breath started to soothe the burn after each strike, another completely different pain overwhelmed me. It was a pulsing pain, a heady almost pleasurable pain. I started to lift my hips in time for each of his smacks, anticipating them, needing them even.

There was something seriously wrong with me. I was sick and twisted, taking enjoyment from the dark debauched givings of my Master.

I turned to look over my shoulder when a faint moan broadcast Master's own arousal. I gasped, my lips parting as I watched him spank me with one hand, his thick cock in his other hand, his fist stroking briskly as he brought himself off. His eyes found mine as his pupils exploded and his cum shot across my back, the thick white cream pumping from him onto the now red skin of my arse. His jaw trembled as he held my gaze, fire spreading over his face as he released another moan of gratification.

He was stunning, the sheer power he projected in that moment of euphoria hypnotising me, holding every single part of me hostage as I watched his satisfaction.

We both stilled when the door swung open and the woman who had tended to me earlier pushed through with a tray in her hands. Her eyes widened on us as she gasped.

"GET OUT!" Master bellowed at her.

"I'm so sorry, Daniel." She flustered as she quickly diverted her eyes and fled back through the door.

"Don't look at me!" Master hissed when my eyes found his again.

He pulled himself back together but I refused his request and watched him quickly tuck himself away. Pain and torment held his expression, his disgust at what had just occurred hurting something inside me.

"I'm sorry I repulse you," I whispered without thinking. I shouldn't have been sorry, I shouldn't have given a damn what he thought of me, but strangely I did. I wanted him to like me, to desire me. There was something about him, no matter how dark his depravity went, that called to me, as though his soul mirrored my own, its call for comfort and understanding denying my hatred towards him.

His eyes snapped to mine and his brow wrinkled. His eyes penetrated deep within me as slight confusion influenced his expression. He was quiet for a moment, his body tight and still as his eyes concentrated on mine. He then gave me a simple nod.

"Clean yourself. I shall be back later and we will start your education."

Education?

He didn't give me a chance to respond before he stormed from the room. His anger controlled his posture, his shoulders pulled back, the thick muscle of them straining the expensive material of his shirt. His backside was firm, the taut fabric of his trousers showcasing his tight buttocks.

I lowered my eyes to the floor as I sat back on my heels, disgusted with myself for checking him out.

"What the fuck is wrong with you?" I asked myself as the portly woman once more appeared in the doorway.

She gave me a small smile. "I've left the soup to warm whilst you take a shower."

I nodded and pulled myself up, allowing her to lead me into the bathroom. I watched her as she pre-warmed the water and collected a few things in readiness for me.

"What's your name?"

She turned to me, her expression troubled and full of lost hope. "Pauline."

I smiled back at her. "Well, thank you, Pauline."

She frowned as she slipped her hand under the spray of water to check the temperature. "What for?"

"For showing me kindness. For treating me as a human and not a dog. For helping me."

She swallowed heavily but shook her head. "Do not let my care confuse you. I am ordered to do these things, none of them are from my own compassion. You are stock, Mae, and I must treat you as such."

My stomach plummeted at her words and tears burnt my eyes. Did no one in this place care? Were they all on a mission to hurt me? My heart ached when I realised that my final days on this earth would be surrounded by people who hated me, people who neither liked nor cared for me.

I nodded and stepped into the shower, releasing her of her discomfort. I waited until the sound of the door closed before I slid to the floor and released the torrent of unhappiness that choked my throat.

Despair and resignation brought frantic sobs. I wished for the progression of my cancer, hoped for its end to relieve me. As though empathising, my brain throbbed in reply, letting me know it was the only thing on my side.

It was with me, the tumour feeding from me, the only thing that needed me. The only thing that could grant me an escape from this nightmare and I prayed for it to hurry the fuck up.

Chapter Nine

'It is the teaching that prepares us, not the lesson.'

"Feed from it, Mae." His voice was tight, the timbre to it a deep rasp as though my pain was his pleasure. "Let the sensation take you higher."

How the fuck did he expect me to *take it higher* when every single inch of my skin blazed, my body already soaring with awareness?

"I can't," I sobbed out. "Please, no more."

He was relentless, the lash of the whip on my back severe and gruelling. "Shut down your mind, lamb. You should be accustomed to this, the slice of your soft skin, the flow of blood beyond your body. You are merely a vessel, a holding for something that carries the pain around your body. Set it free, Mae. Release the pain with the spill of your blood."

What the fuck was this guy on? He was crazy; a freak against nature.

"Would you like to swap places? Show me how it should be done? Maybe my skin is too thin, you know, or maybe I'm just a chicken." I ground out, my temper hanging on by a thread and giving me courage to rant.

He stilled immediately and I grimaced. Oh Christ, I'd upset him again.

I sighed in preparation but my eyes widened when he spluttered. I was too scared to remove my forehead from the floor but his deep chuckle shocked me. I wouldn't have ever had him down as a chuckler, however it lit something inside me and I started to giggle with him.

"Your skin is too thin?" he mocked. "What the bloody hell, Mae?"

I shrugged as laughter rendered me heavy. Unable to move my head due to the hard laughter, I turned my face into the cement floor. "Heck yeah, I'm quite delicate, you know?"

I think I may have lost my mind right then. My own blood was trickling past my face, the copper stench of my life assaulting my nostrils. An absolute nutter was stripping the skin from my back bit by bit and the pain running through me was horrendous; yet, there I was laughing so hard I gained a cramp in my side.

He plonked his backside onto the floor beside me as his laughter took him. I turned my head and looked at him. He was beautiful, his merriment morphing his usual strictness into a carefree expression. Relaxation and happiness suited him, constructed his face into sheer perfection.

His laughter subsided and his eyes found mine. An odd chuckle shook his chest randomly as his humour disappeared and something quite different overtook him. His face relaxed, his eye colour deepened, his chest lifted and fell heavily and his lips parted slightly.

My lungs squeezed tight, holding the air inside. I was terrified to breathe in case it spoilt the moment, took his softness away.

I stared at him, my brow lowering with the pain in his eyes. His tongue darted out and traced the contour of his bottom lip, but his dark eyes never left mine.

"Why didn't you accept treatment?"

His question caught me off guard and I stiffened. I blinked in surprise and swallowed the lump that had formed in my throat. I didn't answer him; he didn't need to know why I had refused every offer at extending my life expectancy.

He didn't grow angry at my refusal as I thought he would, he just continued to gaze at me, confusion and sadness possessing his scrutiny.

"Has life really been that cruel, Mae?"

My eyes dropped to the floor and I regained my stance, my knees and forehead touching the cold concrete floor, my arms stretched out before me and my back arched in readiness for my punishment.

The heavy atmosphere threatened to consume me as I closed my eyes and awaited his continuation of torture. I was pleading for him to take me away from the anguish cut deep and free the thoughts running through my mind. He was correct with one aspect of his lesson; it did take me away from myself, it did allow liberation to my mind, taking the worry of death and the preparation of upcoming pain to disappear under his rule.

"Please," I choked out.

His anger with my diversion physically took over the room. I heard him shuffle to his feet, his breath hissing as he sucked it angrily through his teeth.

"You think you can still deny me, lamb? Refuse my demands?"

I winced as a tear slid free when he brought the whip back down more severely than before. My eyes burnt with each further blow, his fury powering his brutalisation. "You will succumb, Mae. You will give me everything, even your thoughts."

He won then, when my mind could take no more. Numbness took me into oblivion; detachment seized my mind and freed me. I sighed as another strike eased the pain, cooled the agony.

I smiled softly, memories of my mum taking the pain and giving me comfort as I once again sang gently with her, the lyrics soothing to my distress; her warm, happy smile giving me peace.

I hadn't realised the torture had stopped. I hadn't noticed Master had ceased his obstinate persecution. I just sang softly, serenity flooding me as my mother's voice echoed around me as we once again sang together.

I remained there; my forehead on the floor, my knees aching from the cold concrete and my bare behind stuck high for a long time.

I didn't move, even when Pauline started to cleanse the welts covering my back. She didn't speak, nor acknowledge me but her soft humming lulled me into further isolation, my emotions and thoughts belonging to no one, not even myself.

The way it had always been. The way it would be, right up until the end.

I blew out a breath as he circled me, his hands tucked in his trouser pockets, his shirt sleeves rolled to the elbows. "This is the stance you will exhibit when your Master instructs you to take the *Sula* position."

If I dared, I would have rolled my eyes. I couldn't help but feel this was all a waste of time. I didn't have long enough to be anyone's *property,* we both knew it and I just found the whole education pointless and ridiculous.

His foot nudged my legs further apart, demanding absolute perfection. I bit my lip as my predictable temper rose. I was laid flat on my back, naked, my arms by my side, palms up and legs open, displaying my body fully. The aim of this stance was to humiliate, to drill in the understanding that I was someone's possession to do as they pleased with.

"Master," I whispered, asking permission to speak quietly. He huffed but authorised me to continue with a nod. "If I may, why... what is the point of this?"

He frowned and tilted his head. "This is what will be expected of you, Mae. Your complete submission and acquiescence."

"Yes," I continued as I looked up at him. "I understand that but..."

"But?" he urged when I hesitated.

"But well, we both know this is a waste of time." His expression of bewilderment encouraged me. "I won't... be here long enough to even be sold."

Darkness shrouded his face. I gulped at the anger radiating from him. His jaw clenched as he dropped to crouch beside me. "You will cease these thoughts,

Mae. You no longer own your own thoughts. They are mine, and I won't tolerate them."

I squinted at him. "I'm sorry, but my thoughts are there in my head whether I like it or not. You can't stop yourself from thinking, Master."

"I appreciate that, lamb. However, you will no longer see this... illness as it is. You've accepted it, I understand that. Nevertheless, it won't make an ounce of difference."

What the hell?

My mouth opened and closed in shock and I shook my head. "Of course it will make a difference. It's too late now."

I gasped when he snatched my chin in his fingers and twisted my face towards him. "Will you listen for once? I asked you to stop with this topic. It is no longer up for discussion, I forbid it."

Oh well, that was it then – he forbid it!

"But why?" I could sense his fury growing with each question I posed but I couldn't stop. I couldn't understand him and it was this that drove the most disturbing confession from him yet. "Why do you care?"

He scoffed this time, the familiar cruel smile rendering me still in preparation to his words. "Why do I care?" He shook his head slowly and pressed his face nearer to mine. I shivered as his breath once again tickled my ear, the hint of mint from his morning brush tickling my senses. "I care because you are something quite special, Mae. Your beauty, your body, each are worthy of the highest bidder."

My heart sped up as my stomach plummeted with his next revelation. "You are worth a great deal of money to me. You are already on £500,000. And the bidding matures with every moment you succumb to the cruelty. Can you imagine just how much you will be worth fully trained? Your exquisite little cunt is worth at least a million..." I whimpered when he pressed even closer, though the action seemed impossible with his already close proximity. "... dead or alive."

I squeezed my eyes closed, desperately attempting to block the tears as he stood up and walked away.

I rolled over when the door closed behind him, then curled up and cried. Cried for his hatred, and cried for his disgust.

And sobbed for the end to come.

Chapter Ten

'Submit to suffering to find the promise of better.'

My nipples pebbled, the bud of them swollen and rigid as his wet mouth sucked hard on them. His tongue traced around them slowly, the tip flicking occasionally, triggering a jolt of heat into my belly. My fingers found his thick lustrous hair, curling into his dark mane as I pulled him closer, refusing him any escape.

I moaned, my back arching when his teeth teased me, his gentle bite causing a storm between my legs, arousal dampening me in readiness for him.

As though he was aware, his fingers found my warmth, sinking deep into my pussy to feed the need. I pushed against him, eager for more, desperate for him to bate the fire raging inside me.

"Please..." I begged as I bucked into him.

"You're so beautiful when you want me, lamb. So God damned delicious that I need to taste you."

I groaned as his lips trailed down my body, heat following behind his touch. He paused on my stomach, his tongue tracing the edge of my navel. I was going crazy with need, bursting with lust and desire. Gripping his head lightly, I directed him between my thighs. His deep chuckle made me smile; it was so deep and masculine, lighting my desire into an unbearable longing. "God damn it, Daniel. Will you stop torturing me, I need to come."

"Mmm," he murmured, the wisp of his breath teasing my pussy. "You need to come on my tongue, lamb."

"Yes, yes I do."

I cried out in surprise when his teeth clamped my clit lightly, electricity bursting from the bite into my brain. His tongue eased the sting, the flat of it dragging across the tip of the stimulated tissue, generating a deep growl to echo in my throat.

"Fuck, lamb. I love it when you make that sound. Makes my cock throb."

I couldn't wait any longer, the need was too intense. "I need you inside me, I need your cock in me. Please Daniel, please fuck me."

He reared up. My eyes widened on him as he bore his teeth and snarled at me. His eyes filled with hatred. "You filthy-mouthed whore."

I gasped as his fist struck my cheek....

I jolted upright, the hammering in my chest causing me to place my hand on my breastbone to check my heart hadn't actually come through in fright. Sweat tickled my eyes. I pulled a trembling hand across them, wiping away the sting as I searched the dark room.

A dream. Just a dream.

I flopped back on the mattress, the deep luxurious softness enveloping me and calming me immediately. I flung the duvet off in an attempt to cool my raging body. Every single one of my nerves was on fire, the tiny hairs on my body reared up in yearning for a chill to soothe the heat clogging my pores.

I closed my eyes as my own arousal hit my nostrils. I knew I had been on the brink of an orgasm, my stimulated body verified the fact. My belly ached with need as my pussy felt heavy and wet. My nipples were hard, yet it was nothing to do with the sudden drop in temperature.

Memories of the dream flashed behind my eyes, deepening the throb in my veins, encouraging more dampness from my dripping pussy.

I hated myself as I laid my hand on my breast, frowning at the foreign sensation as my own touch lit a path of fire through my excited body. I'd never touched myself before, it had always been something that revolted me, turned my stomach; anything sexual usually made my skin crawl. But right then I felt like I would die if I didn't release the pressure building everywhere; it was painful, every fibre of me stimulated.

As though on instinct, my body telling me what to do, I twisted my nipple in my fingers, the roll of pleasure from it causing me to gasp loudly. My hips lifted as my sex tingled in gratitude to the caress. I bit on my lower lip as my hand slid down my body, seeking the hot flesh of myself. Swallowing heavily I ran my finger over myself, the swollen nerve pulsing in delight when I skimmed my clit. A deep shudder ripped through me as I ran my finger back over with a little more pressure. I released a muffled moan as my lips pressed together firmly and my hips pushed against my finger, encouraging me to move harder and faster.

Nature took over, the urge in me driving my masturbation into a frenzied race for relief. My throat started to close in as my eyes shut tight and I recalled the feel of Master's hot breath on the inside of my thighs.

Heaviness dragged my body, the tension in my muscles crippling as the force of my approaching orgasm apprehended me.

"Remove your hand now!"

I stilled immediately, the closure of my eyes hiding the rush of blood to my cheeks as the shame and horror of being caught touching myself immobilised my body and solidified the air in my lungs. I lay completely still, not even daring to remove my hand as fear held me captive.

"I shall not ask again, lamb."

I slowly opened my eyes and risked a glance towards him. His huge frame was silhouetted against the light from the hallway. In my pleasure-seeking I'd even missed the pouring of light into the room, oblivious in my blissful mind state that I was no longer alone.

Dread and embarrassment rendered me stupid. "I..." I what? I was reckless, I knew that much, but anything else was suddenly unavailable to my brain. "Uhh..."

I flinched when his teeth clashed together, his jaw tightening in anger at my ludicrous response. "Uhh?" he mocked. "Uhh?" The anger in his tone wasn't lost on me.

I grimaced when he took a step closer, eating up the little oxygen in the room with his fury. He stormed the rest of the space between us causing me to jolt when he suddenly bent over me, his face an inch from mine. His eyes were narrow but blazing, his teeth gnawed furiously on his bottom lip as his nostrils flared in his attempt to regain composure. His chest pressed against mine as his large pulls of air heaved his rib cage.

He seemed to be struggling with himself. Uncertainty flashed over his expression as his brows indented slightly. His breathing deepened when his eyes fell from my gaze and stilled on my mouth. He blinked at me and swallowed. "I'm almost desperate for you to spill offensiveness from your mouth so I have a further reason to hurt you."

I didn't understand what he meant. He abhorred my language, yet he seemed to be asking me to curse and swear just to feed his desire to grant me pain.

"You... you want me to swear?" I whispered, my voice breaking. His closeness was feeding something inside me, warming my belly and scorching my veins. I couldn't understand what was happening. His own confusion bewildered me, his struggle brought on my own inner fight. His gaze was warm but his face was cold and stern.

His eyes bulged as they lifted back to mine. "No, that is not what I meant, Mae."

"Then what did you mean?"

My heart stuttered when he closed his eyes. He fell closer, his mouth hovering over mine. His hot breath liquefied my stomach as each of his hands settled gently beside my head, his palms crushing the soft pillow supporting me until his nose was a mere centimetre from the tip of my own.

The sensations he created in my already stimulated body were torturous. My whole body pulsed with need; need for something I couldn't put a name to. I hated myself as I started to pant, my body attempting to dowse the forbidden reaction to him in frequent short spurts of release.

I shuddered when a small growl ripped from his mouth and poured heat over my face, deepening the horrid need inside me. "Please don't," I begged when his hungry eyes gazed back at me

His lips parted and a tremor vibrated his body, his breathing as uncontrollable as mine, his own tiny bursts of air whispering across my lips. His teeth sank into his lip, his battle to control himself nearly at breaking point. I could see it in him, read it in his stare; the need for darkness and animalistic desires rippled from him.

I whimpered and closed my eyes as my body reacted dangerously, my own hunger for carnality taking control. A sob wrenched free when my mind voiced its need without permission. "Hurt me."

It was a whispered plea, a choked murmur that defied everything in me but it was the fact that it wasn't a lie that agonised me, tore my mind into pieces when I realised it was exactly what my body was hunting for. Pain.

His eyes widened further and his breathing halted. I was deeply aware of his arousal pressing into my lower stomach, my words hardening him even further.

Conflict set his stunning face until he appeared to be made of stone, a granite God of raw power and need. The deep colour of his chocolate eyes blackened until they resembled shiny black pebbles reflecting my own stare. His jaw hardened, every single coarse hair on his chin alert and erect as his skin bristled.

I yelped when my body was flipped effortlessly, my knees and elbows bouncing on the mattress. I spluttered when his large hand pressed against the back of my head, pushing my face into the bed without restriction; if it wasn't for the slight crease in the sheet I would have suffocated under the strength of his hold.

I focused on that tunnel of air as my Master hoisted my legs up until my knees locked into position under me, my bottom high and on display as my head and shoulders heaved against the bed.

A shudder ripped through me when I heard the tell-tale sound of a zip being lowered. He wasn't slow, in fact his growl of frustration lit something inside me when he couldn't seem to lower it fast enough. A deep-seated carnal hunger for debauchery and depravity glowed in the room around me, stilling every single inch of me. A shameless want for pain ached inside me, the strength of it thickening my blood. I squeezed my eyes closed when recognition clashed with degradation, but even that struck the match to my arousal. My own mortification turned me on.

I was ill; sick and fucking perverse.

The burn of a slap fired across my right buttock, the sting heightened every single nerve that was already on edge. My teeth vibrated as need and desire overtook.

"Do it," I begged, my voice floating around us, the tone sounding as though it had come from someone else, someone far from who I was. I didn't care anymore, the yearning was too potent. My starved emptiness needed filling quickly, and if that meant I had to ask, then so be it. I would fucking beg if I had to.

His body encompassed me until he was completely mounting me, his huge frame shadowing and eating me alive.

"Ask properly, my little lamb. Ask me for what you need with dignity and manners."

I gulped, desperately trying to hold back the nausea at my own revolting desires. A tear rolled from my eye, just a solitary one as his teeth clamped the soft skin on my neck and he growled, his lust nearly ripping a chunk of flesh in his haste for me to answer so he could give us both what we needed. A throb so fierce ached my body at the pain his teeth brought, but it gave me the courage I needed to deal with... whatever was going on between us.

"Make me cry. Feed me with pain, stop this thirst of need in me..." I shivered as I felt his cock slip between my buttocks, a deep groan alerting me to the fact that he was as close to insanity as I was. "...please, Master."

That was all it took. I arched and screamed when he thrust urgently inside me. His length filled me to burning point and his width seemed to tear me apart from the inside. My slick arousal had eased his passage but he still ripped me. The sudden tear inside brought forth another scream when a scorch of pain shot through me. It felt like I'd lost my virginity, the sharp singe triggering the release of sobs.

I wept. But not for the pain. I sobbed for the delight coursing through my body. I cried at the bliss that made my eyes roll. I howled at the utter feeling of euphoria as my Master's punishing thrusts tore me to pieces but made my body vibrate in ecstasy. And I wept for my sanity.

I screamed at the approaching orgasm as my Master powered into me mercilessly. His fingers were as punishing as his fucking as they dug deep into my hips, each grunt he voiced forcing his grasp harder and harder.

"You fuck like you sing, lamb...." He pushed my face further into the bed as he sped up his pounding, his cock driving deeper and deeper. I was struggling to breathe but that only heightened each sensation coursing through me. "...fucking bewitching!"

His words frayed the thread I was managing to hold onto. My mind burst as my climax exploded. My soul shifted away from my body for a matter of milliseconds but I watched in awe as I viewed Master and his slave fucking like animals, their grunting and sweat filling the air, their clawing and painful joining mesmerising and enthralling.

Master reared back as I felt his cum swamp my womb, the warmth snapping me back to reality. He roared out a deep groan, his fingernails cutting into my flesh and forcing blood to seep from me as his body jerked and bucked inside me.

I closed my eyes, screwing them up in horror as my body rejoiced at dragging the seed from my owner, pulling his desire from him and into me.

However, my joy was short lived.

He pulled out, leaving a chill to seep into me. I dared not move. Now the arousal had disappeared I wasn't sure how he would react.

"Well." He sighed heavily. I had the strange feeling he was angry with me but his fight to control it confused me further. "Well, that scratched an itch."

My eyes popped open and I stared at the mattress as the door closed behind him. "That scratched an itch," I repeated in bewilderment. "What the fuck?"

I dropped flat onto the bed, uncertainty flowing through my sated body. I cringed when I felt Master's sperm dribble from inside me, coating my thighs and the bed in... him.

What the fuck had just happened? I was struck dumb as the truth of my body's own betrayal rendered me still. I had given myself over eagerly, in fact I had fucking begged for it, to someone who repulsed me, a monster who had devoured my soul on his first storm into my life.

And now, as I accepted my own sickness, his unique personal storm ripped my soul from within me once again.

Chapter Eleven

"A monster hides his true nature.'

"M…Miss Mae…"

I groaned in reply. It was obvious Frank had been sent to wake me. The sunlight trying to blare through my eyelids was strong and already warm, confusing me since it was January – well I thought it was anyway. Time seemed to have gone to pot in there. Winter sun was never this warm in England, or maybe we weren't even in the UK – all the window offered was lots of green grass and that gave me no indication as to my location. I hadn't been outside in such a long time and my heart ached at the thought of fresh air.

"Mae," Frank persisted. I smiled internally when one of his large hands tried to shake me awake. Although Frank was a giant, his touch and rocking were extremely gentle, almost as though he was frightened of breaking me.

"Frank, please. Not today, my head hurts."

I could sense his unease. He had been given an order and I was under no illusions what would happen to him if he didn't carry it out to perfection. Master was a stickler for perfection. "B…b…but…"

I prised my eyes open, his distress making my stomach hurt. I couldn't work out what it was about Frank that I liked. He was a huge wall of muscle, his face was hard, his eyes even harder, yet he had stuck up for me with the Demi-whore and he would never understand how much it meant to me. No one had ever stuck up for me other than Spud – apart from Daniel with Liam; however, that didn't count any longer. So yeah, it was just Frank and Spud that held that spot now.

Vomit surged up my throat when Frank blurred before me. My forehead screeched in pain, violent light exploding through my brain with the effort of focussing. "Please tell Master that..." I blew out a steadying breath. "I can't, Frank. Not today."

I turned over as gently as possible so as not to grieve my brain any further. My stomach rolled at the movement but I managed to fight it, pulling in a firm breath to counteract the twist in my gut and my head.

He scurried round the bed. I could sense him staring at me worriedly. "Mae, w...we have visitors for breakfast. You m...must."

"Visitors?" I made the effort to look at him. He deserved that. The poor man had taken a beating for me, the least I could do was give him my respect.

He nodded rapidly, his expressionless eyes fixed on mine. "Yes, you must a...accompany M...Master and..." He scowled and shook his head when he realised he'd nearly slipped up. I had better not be accompanying Demi.

"Frank?"

He scowled, more to himself than me. His lips pursed in annoyance as he stared at me. Sudden light hit his eyes before he smiled at me. "L...Look Mae." His large hands lifted, dragging a large piece of silver material in front of his body. "B...beautiful. You'll l...look beautiful, Mae."

Shock and humour brought forward a giggle. "Well, Frank. I must say you look stunning." He blinked at me then looked down at himself. He held the dress to his body as though he was spending fun time with girlfriends in the changing rooms at Monsoon. "That is so your colour." I winced when another giggle bounced around my skull, banging on my front lobe.

He chuckled and swayed his hips playfully. "I do, Miss Mae. Yes, I d...do."

"Oh, Frank." I smiled and sighed as I pulled at my aching body and slowly let my feet drop to the floor. The deep cushioning carpet shot sensation up my legs and spine, torturing my head further but Frank deserved my obedience, and hopefully soon my friendship. "I like you, Frank." He blushed furiously when I reached on my tiptoes and whispered the words in his ear. His face dropped to the floor but I didn't miss his large smile.

"A...And I like you, Mae."

The simple declaration stilled me and I sighed sadly. "Thank you."

"W...Why so sad? We're now f...friends. You s...should be happy."

I rested my hand on his cheek and smiled. "You have no idea how happy it makes me to be your friend. No one ever wants to be my friend. So, thank you."

He stared at me, his eyes glinting with what looked like anger. "Why?"

I started to shake my head in confusion at his question but the act caused further sickness to creep up my throat. "Why?"

"W...w...why d...does no one l...like y...you?" His indignation aggravated his stutter, making him almost incomprehensible.

I broke down the words in my head so as not to offend him by asking him to repeat himself. "I don't know, Frank. But that's okay, I'm okay with it. Don't worry. You mustn't be upset, I like my own company."

He blinked rapidly, his Adam's apple bobbing furiously as he tried to control his upset. My heart lurched. No one had ever held any emotion whatsoever about my life. I was Mae Swift, the freak who had no friends, no family and no life. That's how it was, how it had always been since my early teens. However, watching my 'friend' hurt made me love him even more.

"Okay." I spoke suddenly, making Frank jolt. "Let's try this dress on."

He nodded as I rapidly changed the subject, his face showing the same enthusiasm as mine at the swift diversion.

He pushed the dress towards me then bent to pick up a small square box that he must have placed on the chair before he woke me. He looked worried, his brow furrowed and his teeth chewing the corner of his mouth as he held it towards me. His hands shook as a scowl tightened his face. "M...Master says you m...must wear this t...too."

His blush alerted my senses. I frowned even though the effort of such a simple facial expression hurt my head in various places. I took the box from him and lifted the lid.

My eyes bulged and I stared in horror at the scrap of silver lace laid perfectly on a pillow of silk. The box dropped from my grasp as I hooked the fabric around my little finger and held it up in front of my face. Crotchless knickers. Expensive crotchless knickers. *Very* expensive crotchless knickers.

Oh fucking shit!

"I can't wear these!" I barked at Frank like it was his own personal request that I create the wonderful draft between my legs.

He cringed and directed his blazing cheeks to the floor. "M...Master says... just those under the d...dress, M...Mae."

"Fuck that! I don't fucking care what his royal highness wants. He wants me in them, then he can fucking staple the bastard things to my arse."

I ignored Frank's horrified look and stomped towards the dresser that had been loaded with different items of clothing. The amount of things that had been systematically placed in each drawer made me laugh out loud. I wouldn't have time to ever wear a quarter of them, never mind the whole collection of designer garments.

I pulled out the item I needed and turned back to Frank. "I suggest you leave now, Frank. I don't want you getting in trouble for witnessing my insubordination."

He gulped as panic disfigured his innocent face. "P...Please Mae."

I shook my head slowly, not bothering to look at him whilst I hunted for a specific item. "Leave." My sharp tone made him jump but I refused to get this gentle man into any more trouble because of me. He needed to leave then there would be no comeback on him.

I glanced at him as he made his way to the door with his eyes on his feet. His worry made me contemplate whether I was right to do what I had in mind, but anger flowed through my veins. I refused to succumb to Daniel's sick fucking desires. The bastard wanted my soul then he'd get it, along with my spirit and wrath.

My wide eyes swallowed my surroundings eagerly as I followed Pauline down the long hallway. This was a completely different part of the house than I'd been allowed access to before. Our journey through many different corridors in the huge manor already had my toes curling and my heels screaming at the soreness from walking in the impossibly high heels that had been supplied with my outfit.

Pauline had gawked at me when I presented myself to her. The silver dress I'd been ordered to wear was exquisite – unfortunately. The beautiful, light silky material hugged each of my curves deliciously, skimming over any excess lumps and bumps my hips and arse stowed. The lack of straps and the way the material accentuated my breasts, instead of usually focussing on my jutting collarbones, complimented the length of my neck, almost as though its style deceived the human eye. The delicate flow of the hem line skimmed over my thighs, not quite touching my knees but not too short as to show what was underneath. Very sexy, but classy. Admitting that my Master appreciated style left a bitter taste in my mouth, and I hated the fact that I'd been in actual awe at the transformation in the mirror.

Cosmetics and stupidly expensive scents had decorated the dresser in my room in preparation for this so called visit. Yet, each one of those items had helped transform my body into something quite, even if I admitted it myself, something quite stunning. The ugly freak no longer stared at me through the looking glass. A striking, elegant young woman now masked the hideousness. However, I wasn't sure if I appreciated that fact or not.

Anguish and dread bubbled violently in my stomach, my head throbbed until my vision became ghostly and cloudy and my heart rate threatened to send me into a coma. My rebelliousness now hung heavy in my gut. Had it been a wise thing? I highly doubted it now my rage had diminished.

"Pauline." I grasped her elbow, halting her wide strides towards our destination. She turned to me, her face questioning. "I need to go back."

Her eyes widened. "You can't, we're already late."

"But, you don't..."

A door swung open in front of us and I froze when Master's cold stare landed on us. His eyes met mine before they slowly dropped to study his possession.

His brows rose slowly, his chest seemed to heave as his teeth sank into his bottom lip.

He took my breath. He stood before me in a morning suit, his wide chest encased in an exclusive grey two piece. A silver tie complimented his pale blue shirt and the way his matching grey trousers hugged his strong thighs made my mouth water. His dark, hair was styled to perfection, sweeping off his forehead and rebelling against the messy cut on top. I shook my head, deleting whatever message my eyes were sending to my pussy.

He swallowed heavily before raising his gaze back to my face. "At last, lamb. I wondered if you had refused my request and decided to dine out tonight."

I stared at him in astonishment. "Your humour leaves me cold, Master."

Damn my fucking mouth. Why the hell couldn't I just bite back my thoughts? His face darkened as his fingers curled into a tight fist. His gaze shot to Pauline. "Leave us."

She nodded in reply to his seething order. Her eyes met mine when she turned. I wasn't sure if she displayed dismay or amazement at my stupid outburst.

He slowly shut the door behind him. My eyes burnt with the strengthening of my headache. Nausea threatened to embarrass me further but I knew my Master had no interest in excuses.

He stalked towards me, his furious eyes on mine. "Nadu, Mae."

I bit my tongue this time. I was already on his Christmas naughty list, I didn't want to make the bad birthday one too. I gathered the front of my skirt in my hands and fell to my knees before him. The thump on the floor ricocheted trauma around my sensitive skull and I winced as pain fired through my temples.

His firm grasp on my hair made the wave of approaching unconsciousness highly desirable. I cringed, swallowing back the bile. I gasped when he dropped to his haunches before me, and with a finger under my chin, directed my gaze to his. "What must I do to acquire your obedience, Mae?"

My mouth fell open with his question. I hadn't been expecting that. His query had been soft and truthful, as though he wanted to earn my compliance. I blinked but faced him with as much confidence as I could muster. "Let me go home."

His brow quirked, the action lifting a corner of his lips with it. His amusement hurt. It shouldn't, but I hated his mockery of me, another cruel taunt to add to the very long list.

He tutted then tightened his hold on my hair, making me yelp faintly. "I will never understand you, lamb. Time after time I offer leniency, yet every time you choose to renounce it."

He pushed me back as his hand left my hair. I slapped my hands on the floor to stop myself falling over. "For your waywardness, you will enter behind me on your hands and knees."

I barked out a forbidden laugh. "What the hell?"

His palm smashed across my cheek before I could even register what it was. My face flung the other way when his other hand slapped the opposite cheek. I knew I must have looked like a damn clown with two glowing bright red cheeks.

I glared at him but the pain that overwhelmed my body brought on my swift surrender. I couldn't cope with any more knocks to my head. The pain was becoming uncontrollable and I knew without my medication I wouldn't be able to hold back the encroaching sickness.

"Fine," I spat out.

He smirked at me. "I have no care whether you are *fine* with it or not, you will do it."

Arrogant bastard.

I held his stare and straightened my back as I manoeuvred onto all fours beside him. He didn't show any gratitude or even appreciation at my obedience. I couldn't win. He took great delight in chastising me but it was very rare I received his compliments.

He took a step towards the door. I shuffled beside him, the skirt of my dress making me stumble until I found a rhythm. His long fingers hung by his side. I could almost picture a leash in his hand.

I groaned internally when my bloody attitude refused to be silent. "Woof." It left my mouth quietly but not quietly enough.

His steps stuttered beside me and he released a deep sigh.

"I'm sorry, Master," I muttered quickly. I wasn't really but I couldn't cope with any more head abuse.

I glanced up at him when he shook his head slowly. His eyes dropped to mine and I fought the excitement in my belly when I was greeted to amusement on his face. He pinched the bridge of his nose and groaned. "Whatever am I going to do with you, lamb?"

I remained silent. He didn't expect an answer to his statement, and I didn't offer one.

His hand paused on the door handle to the room he had come from. "You will remain silent. You will refuse eye contact with anyone unless requested. You *will behave.* You will allow anything asked of you..."

"Whoa..."

He turned sharply. I shuddered when his fingers spread across the nape of my neck and squeezed. "I repeat..." he hissed as he tightened his grip, making my brain swell with the pressure. I whimpered when lightning fired across my vision, huge strikes of electricity alerting me to the fact that we would soon have a problem on our hands.

"Master..." I whimpered as I tried to alert him to the direction my illness was taking that particular day.

"Shut – up. I will no longer accept your unruliness. You no longer have thoughts or decisions. You are controlled. You are a robot awaiting orders." I squealed when his grip constricted. "Is that understood?"

Well I wasn't going to say no, was I? I mumbled a yes. It was all I could manage under the terrifying ghosts dictating my vision. My brain was beginning to vibrate, the tell-tale sign that I was going to lose all motor skills very shortly.

I didn't want to embarrass my Master when it happened, when my tumour declared its presence so chillingly. Yet, I wanted to humiliate him at the same time. He didn't deserve to be alerted to the potential catastrophe of what would happen to me.

His hand slid into my hair. I squealed when he seized the roots at the nape of my neck and twisted them. I was no longer allowed to follow. I was dragged alongside him instead. My scalp burnt under the grip of his long fingers.

I kept my eyes trained at the floor. I wasn't even sure I wanted to see what greeted me in the room. The deep red carpet gave me all the interest I needed, its hue the same deep crimson that flowed from each of my many defacements. I was mesmerised by it.

I swallowed and squeezed my eyes closed when a thousand insects appeared to slither across my path, forewarning me that the hallucinations were imminent and delirium threatened to take my sanity.

"Master," I gasped as panic overwhelmed me. My heart rate increased rapidly. He would not be happy with my behaviour if I upset his guests. "Master, please."

He hissed through his teeth and dug his fingers into a section of soft flesh on the side of my neck causing a severe pain to surge down my backbone, each groove of my spine screaming in agony.

Right, that decided my fate. There would be no more attempts to warn him. He would get the shock value along with whoever else was in the room.

Master led me over to what looked like a Perspex podium; a tall clear column of plastic topped with a large sturdy looking disc of thick transparent plastic similar to the base. Okay. Why did that particular piece worry me?

I jerked back when he pulled on my hair, declaring his demand for me to stand before the odd piece of furniture. "Get up!" he hissed quietly through his teeth.

"You're actually putting me on a pedestal?" I scoffed.

The potency of his anger clogged my throat, making my body hypersensitive and my breathing still. Why the hell couldn't I just shut up? What was wrong with me?

I sizzled angrily in his hard hold when he hoisted me up and yanked me to his side. "I will not allow your rudeness in front of my guests, Mae. You won't like the consequences of your actions if you humiliate me."

I rolled my eyes and huffed. Master frowned at me as a nasty bite to my brain caused me to sway in his hold. "Is your tumour giving you grievance?"

"Not as much as you!" I bit back.

Holy fucking shit, Mae. I must have had a death wish. Well, actually, I did.

"Keep pushing, lamb." I swallowed at the cold smile he gave me. It seeped inside me and made me shiver involuntarily. His smirk grew wider as the effect he had on me presented itself clearly through my body. "You have a right to be scared." He leaned further into my ear, his teeth clamping quite delicately over my soft lobe. "I will crush you in a heartbeat should your insolence prove extra difficult this morning. And don't think the loss of earnings associated with your death will bother me, I'm sure half a million won't put a dent in my grocery budget."

"You arsehole."

My head bashed against the plastic pillar when Master's fist exploded my cheekbone. Fire surged from the base of my spine and up my vertebrae, bursting excruciating agony behind my eyes.

My Master was one lucky son of a bitch. His violence halted my encroaching lunacy. The beating he gave me snatched my consciousness, therefore removing any threat my tumour had planned for me.

Darkness swallowed me and the pain granted me feverish bleak oblivion.

Chapter Twelve

'Sometimes honesty is far worse than lies.'

I sensed him beside me but I kept my eyes closed before I allowed him to set his fury free on me. His anger was tangible, coating me in the thick substance of rage. His heavy breathing was rhythmic and hypnotic, lulling me into a false sense of comfort.

My head seemed better, although a dull throb pulsed in my temples; however, I sensed that was more to do with the hammering I'd received for yet another of my loose-tongued errors.

My face felt only slightly swollen which mystified me. I'd have thought after the furious pelts he'd rained on me that I would have resembled an overweight woman with an addiction to Botox.

Okay, so not too bad considering what my body had once again fought against.

I inhaled deeply and peeked through one eye. Master sat in a chair beside my bed, his elbows resting casually on his knees as he leaned towards me. I was shocked to find him in pale blue jeans and a white T-shirt, the soft cotton clinging to every delectable muscle across his impressive chest.

He continued to stare at me. I couldn't get an indication of his mood from his expression, his eyes were cold as usual but his face was lax and soft. "Welcome back, Mae."

"Hi." I cracked open my other eye, amazed to find my vision completely fine. I had expected either my Glioma to blur it, or damage to my retinas from Master's hits. From the slight sting in my arm though, I knew Dr Galloway had been called to tend to me.

Master took a deep breath and leaned back into the chair, crossing one ankle over his thick thigh and linking his fingers together in his lap. I couldn't help dropping my gaze to appreciate the view. I hated how perfect he was. It made it difficult to breathe as my heart and head balked with hatred, but my belly and pussy burnt in need.

His intense study of me became uncomfortable, his deep gaze suffocating and devouring. I cleared my throat and shuffled up the bed until my back rested against the headboard. My body was once again covered by the simple pink slip. It felt strange to be comforted by an item of clothing, yet the nightdress did exactly that. It felt like it belonged to me, and there, where nothing belonged to me, it gave me a sliver of reassurance and solace, as stupid as that sounded.

He sighed again and twisted his lips, thoughts and contemplations racing through his eyes. He clicked his tongue rapidly on his teeth as his eyes narrowed on me. "How long do you have?" It was asked so bluntly that a lump formed in my throat. If he'd have smacked me with a cricket bat it wouldn't have made much difference to the shock factor.

I squirmed and dropped my eyes. "I'm not sure..." I gulped but powered on. "I'm not sure that is any of your concern."

His chin lifted slightly but other than that he showed no signs of offence with my answer. "Ahh, but that is where you are wrong, my little lamb. It has everything to do with me."

"Well, I'm sorry but I beg to differ," I replied indignantly. It had absolutely bollocks all to do with him. I was slightly pleased at myself when I managed to keep those last few words in my head without them spewing from my mouth

He chuckled softly and sighed with a hint of sadness. I frowned when he reached down and picked something off the floor. The corner of the bed restricted my view and I couldn't see what he had until he held it up with one finger, exactly like I had. Oh dear.

I gulped and hesitantly lifted my eyes from the silk knickers I had refused to wear, to Master's eyes. One of his eyebrows was elevated, giving him an amused expression but the infuriation in his eyes chilled my bones.

He bent yet again and I squeezed my eyes closed. I didn't need to see what he had retrieved this time.

"Open your eyes, lamb."

My stomach turned over. I refused to witness what he held. If I didn't look then he wasn't holding the proof of my misbehaviour. "I'm sorry," I offered without releasing my eyelids from their defensive position. I didn't want to see what furious expression he held whilst swinging those around his other finger, which I had no doubt he would be.

"Now is not a good time for your lack of discipline to exasperate me any further. Open – your – eyes and look at me. Show some courage. I know it's in you, Mae. You've shown it enough times, but unfortunately, always at the wrong times."

The clench in my stomach didn't ease when I relented and opened my eyes; it twisted more when I found each offensive item spinning around each of his forefingers.

His smile was sinister, his blazing eyes fixed on me, sucking the air from my lungs like he had comic book superpowers.

"I'm sorry, "I repeated in a whisper.

He nodded slowly. Initially I thought it was a nod of forgiveness but that soon turned to horror when he muttered three simple words. "Time to play."

I didn't care that I resembled a rabid dog when I started panting in sheer fright. I didn't like the sound of that. It left my fate wide open.

He swung the bright yellow Lycra cycling shorts faster and faster until he flicked his finger and they shot across the space between us and slapped me in the face. "You acquire the privilege to wear those to the next breakfast meeting..." My breath refused to listen to what was coming and gushed the wrong way out making me splutter stupidly. "If you answer my questions truthfully."

Panic set in and I stared at him, my eyes wide and round as my chest heaved.

"However," he continued, "refuse and you get to wear these..." He neatly placed the knickers across one of his thighs, ironing them out smoothly, "...and only these."

"What? No dress?"

He shook his head slowly. "No dress, Mae."

"And if I refuse?" I didn't care if I was riling him. I was tired of playing his games, exhausted with trying to figure out his next move on the board.

He laughed coldly. "Please give me the satisfaction of allowing me to demonstrate that particular choice. There is nothing more delicious that would make my cock hard than watching you swing naked, bleeding and bruised from a chain wrapped around your pretty little neck."

My jaw dropped. "My God. You're just..." I snapped my mouth closed, my brain freaking out at my stubborn will to voice my thoughts.

"Yes, I am *just*." He leaned forward again but this time steepled his fingers and ran the tips of them along his lips. I could sense his excitement and I had no doubt he wished for my denial, the sick fuck.

"Fine," I spat. I didn't need to ask what his first question was, he'd already asked it. "Two months at most."

His lips thinned as a tic twitched in his cheekbone. He nodded. "Why did you refuse the offer of treatment?"

"Master, this really is of no consequence..."

"Answer the damn question, Mae!" he shouted, making me flinch.

I scowled at him, nevertheless I growled out the answer. "Because there's no point."

He eyed me warily. "Oh come on, lamb. There's always purpose."

"Not really."

"No, I apologise but I do not agree. Life is life, whether it be a mere dull existence or a rainbow of brilliant colour. Every heart beats the same as another. Every soul deserves the chance to shine."

"Yet you're willing to snatch life away so easily."

I was surprised by his tolerance to my argument. I had expected his ire at my debate but he spoke as if we were having a casual conversation over coffee.

"Because I have been given that job if you fail to meet the specifications." He was open and forthright, granting me hope to dig deeper.

"I don't understand, Master. Your job?"

He nodded once, his beautiful brown eyes never leaving mine. "Yes. I am an auctioneer."

"An auctioneer of what?" I internally begged him to keep going. His game of interrogation had switched, the topic now him and I was hungry for information, necessity to find out the truth driving me into the danger zone.

He snorted as though I was stupid. "Why, you and other stock, of course."

"Other stock?"

He frowned at me. "Yes. Did you think there was just you in my guardianship?"

"Oh my God. There's more here?"

"You and one other, yes." He shifted forward towards the bed and placed both of his palms on the edge. "You are both stock, objects for the buyers to barter against."

My mouth was too dry. I couldn't seem to form words as my heart galloped in my chest and my stomach threatened to tear up my throat. "I…"

He laughed. "Yes, and you've become quite the booty, so to speak. I'm actually quite amazed at how many bids you have received in the previous three years."

The room swam when my vision blurred, this time having nothing to do with my illness. "Th...Three years?"

The information I had been desperate for sickened me. I wanted to remove the knowledge I held, scorch it from my mind and leave behind a black charred chasm that wouldn't be half as painful as what currently possessed that section of my sanity. There was only one explanation for his revelation and that thought sucked out my soul. I asked the question although I already knew deep down what the answer would be. "How?"

He rolled his eyes but smiled. I flinched when he yanked back the blanket covering me. Scuttling back when he reached out, he growled and wrapped his fingers around my ankle, pulling me back down the bed towards him. I cowered when he lugged up my nightdress.

I gulped when he softly drew his finger along a small scar on the outside of my left thigh. "How did you get this scar, Mae?"

I shook my head. "I... I don't know."

He nodded and gave me a crooked smile, both pride and hilarity glowing across his features. "I do." He ran his finger up and down the tiny one inch silver line. "I gave it to you."

"You gave me many scars, both internally and externally." My unrestricted truth lifted his eyes to mine. A glimpse of pain flickered across his eyes, turning the deep rich brown into a dim hazel tinge. Was it remorse he exhibited or dismay at my recurring careless statements?

"I did. Nevertheless," he continued, "you won't remember me creating it. You were unconscious at the time."

I shivered, horror at what he was saying filling me. "What... what did you do to me after?"

I had no idea what had happened after Daniel had injected some sort of toxin into my veins after he had cruelly taken what he wanted from me. All I could remember after waking in my apartment two days later was how sore my whole body had been. I was too scared to go to the police. I knew they wouldn't appreciate a young girl stupidly going to a stranger's house, dressed like a slut. If I was honest with myself, I knew I would have given Daniel my virginity that night anyway. But I had been foolish, I thought it would have come with romance, softness and gentle caresses. I'd even packed bloody condoms in my bag. In the end it would have been a costly case of me, a wayward teenager with a history of depression, drug abuse and self-harm against a high powered businessman. And let's face it, the house that Daniel had taken me to was not one a mere working class person could have afforded.

It turned out it hadn't even been his house. I had plucked up the courage four days later to cycle past at speed, just for a hint of something, anything to fill the gap in my memories, the gaping black hole he had created in my existence. Then when I had gotten there, a small throng of people were being shown around on an open auction day. How Daniel had acquired the keys to the place was beyond me, but his trouble at entering the correct gate code and inserting the right key in the lock had suddenly made sense.

But by then it was too late. All *evidence* had gone and the internal conflict of my stupidity deterred my desire to report it.

"Oh, don't worry, lamb. I didn't take you again. Although, in truth, I debated it. You were quite something. In spite of this, I like my partners to be sentient."

The conversation was becoming surreal. "Please, just tell me. What did you do?" I practically begged him, although I wasn't sure I wanted to hear the answer.

He blinked softly at me, a faint smile tilting his lips gently. "You're wearing a tracker, Mae."

I fell backwards, my back bouncing off the head of the bed as shock took over and I lost management of my own body. I struggled to breathe, each tiny pocket of air in my lungs rapidly firing up my throat in short little whimpers. Tears congested behind my eyes, stinging my ducts.

My eyes bulged when realisation hit me. Panic saw me scrambling from the bed towards him. He reared back when I grabbed at him, the material of his T-shirt bunching between my fists. "What do you know? How much do you know about...? Do you know? Do you?" I fired hurriedly in desperation.

I winced when his hand encompassed my throat and he pushed me back. "I suggest you hold onto that temper, Mae. Use it on me again and I'll punish you severely."

"But I need to know," I choked out, my voice high and tight as I pushed past the restriction on my voice box. "Please. Do you know?"

"Know?" He narrowed his eyes curiously on me. "Know what, Mae? What are you hiding?"

He obviously didn't know or he wouldn't be asking. I relaxed a little, forcing myself to calm down before he probed any farther into my behaviour. "You've been watching me for three years?"

He relaxed his hold when he sensed my control. "No, like I said, you have a tracker, not a damn internal camera. Why are you so worried, lamb?"

I swallowed. "Wouldn't you be worried if someone had been following you around for three years? I mean, what the fu...heck? You can't do that. It's... it's wrong. So, so wrong."

"Do you think I care about *wrong*?" He laughed loudly, once more mocking me. "Even with your disfigurements, Mae, my clients want you, *need* you. They ache for you, willing to outbid their competition with extraordinary amounts of money."

He leaned forward, a malicious glint in his eyes. "Once a year, each year, I've watched you, lamb. Tracked your location then watched you shop, watched you go to work, and then watched your self-pity through your apartment window. I have viewed you deciding which bottle of wine to treat yourself to each Christmas. It actually saddened me that you bought no gifts or any small luxuries for yourself over the festive period. I saw you get mauled by that fucker of a taxi driver when he thought you would pay for your ride in other ways. I witnessed your tears every Christmas Eve on the stroke of midnight, your huge eyes blinking in time with every single fairy light on your poor excuse for a Christmas tree. I've observed your every breath for five days prior to Christmas each year from my taking until your third year in which you were ready for me."

Each of his words caused another tear to drip from my eyes. My soul deserted me, its weeping too painful to witness. My body gave in and my mind closed down.

Master caught me as I fainted and slid off the bed.

Chapter Thirteen

'Veiled evil exposes true depravity.'

I shuddered when the tickle from the trail of his fingertip across my cheek brought back my consciousness. I didn't want to open my eyes; I didn't want reality to once more pain me. Everything was so fucked up, my whole life corrupted and blurred by lies and selfishness.

For the first time in a very long time I missed my family. I missed the security of my mother's arms, the soft but encouraging smile from my father. Connie's laugh.

"I know you are conscious, Mae. Open your eyes. Your education needs to continue immediately."

I sighed but slowly slid open my eyes. His face came into focus immediately. He was close, his breath warm but far from comforting. "Please," I breathed. "Please let me be. I can't do this anymore."

He didn't laugh as I had expected him to. Instead the tender tilt of his lips and the gentle stroke of his finger caressed my every sense. His eyes locked onto mine with something I couldn't read. It confused me, warping my already delicate thoughts.

His tongue stroked his bottom lip, catching my attention as he brought his finger down the length of my facial scar. "This frustrates me, lamb. Although it doesn't spoil your beauty, it disfigures your spirit."

I swallowed slowly. I didn't like what his touch did to my wild body. The arousal he created infuriated me, turned my body against my mind, repulsing my very own thoughts. My throat closed in as my heart thundered against my breastbone, the knock, knock, knock furious in its demand to be heard. "You took my spirit three years ago. So tell me, Master, how can you see its disfigurement when it's already dead and gone?"

He cocked his head very faintly, his gaze troubled. He twisted his lips and he inhaled deeply as though in serious thought. His touch continued to idolise my mutilation, as if his many strokes over it would heal the damage. "Your spirit is very much alive and passionate. I didn't steal it from you. You tried to give it me willingly, lamb; yet, look at you." His fingers moved around so he could cup my chin and position my face until I was looking at him. "You have fought me every day since you awoke in here. You refuse to relinquish your control. You still curse, you still argue and you still believe."

I scoffed and tried to shake my head out of his hold. "I still believe in what, Master? You tell me I no longer own my own thoughts, my decisions. Yet, here you are telling me the very opposite. Your frequent demands gobble up my individuality. And I know you won't stop until you have devoured every last thought in my head, every single fibre of me and each piece of my mind. So, please enlighten me as to how I still have spirit when your relentless push to drive it from me is becoming more and more difficult to fight against?"

He stared at me. I had already braced my body in preparation for the backlash and annoyingly I cowered when he shot upright, although I blinked in shock when he held out his hand. "Come with me."

"I don't want to." I knew I was in trouble, the next few hours of my life booked in the 'correction centre'. I was tired. My body was exhausted and my mind was weak. I wasn't sure I could withstand any more physical abuse. I knew he would give it me anyway so what did it matter if I goaded him enough into dishing out my punishment in the comfort of my room; at least I would have the butterflies to look at whilst he tried to beat all lucidity out of me.

He rolled his eyes. "See, I told you that your spirit was still in your possession." He thrust his hand further towards me. "Please." I could see his polite request was forced but nonetheless it was there.

I had nothing to lose. His fingers curled around my own when I slipped my tiny hand into his large one. The heat of his grasp when he curled his fingers around mine caused a hard shudder.

Master didn't look at me as he pulled me through the house. It was night time, the darkness outside the windows providing no light in the dimly lit corridors. The eerie silence enveloped us as my eyes roamed the scenery on my journey. There were many paintings hung from the walls, but no personal ones, no family portraits or photographs that would give me any clue to who Master was. Small sconces decorated the wallpaper providing sufficient light to illuminate our passage. Occasional ornaments, lamps and vases full of flowers provided a reprieve against the harsh deep red colour of the décor. But nothing was personal; none of it was a *home*.

He pushed a door and our excursion ended in a huge rustic kitchen. It was square in shape but the many orderly cabinets and cupboards gave it a soft hexagonal appearance. It was hard to explain but the way it had been designed to soften the hard edges and strict contours made it finally feel like a home. The deep smell of many different aromas reminded me of my own childhood; herbs and spices still lingered in the atmosphere, traces of jams and sugars tickled my nostrils as remnants of the evening's dinner were exposed in the yeasty scent only slightly eclipsing the faint smell of garlic.

"I like this room." It slipped from my mouth easily while a smile ghosted my lips when cosiness surrounded me.

Master didn't acknowledge my words, he just pulled me across the cool tile floor into a door at the far end. We carried on down some steep stone steps, the air chilling and dampness rising considerably the further we descended.

My mouth fell open when my eyes took in row after row of dusty bottles. They were arranged methodically around the room, each bowed shelf groaning under the weight of coloured glass and vintage wine.

He pulled me through endless lines of different wine until he briskly halted and turned into another room. It was small, maybe six foot square with an incredibly low ceiling and brick walls. I gawped at the endless varieties of whisky. There were hundreds of various shaped bottles, each their own distinct colour and style.

Master reached up high and pulled a dusty bottle from the very top shelf. He dropped my hand and swept off the dust, faintly blowing at the label to make sure he was holding the precise one he wanted. He remained silent as he gave himself a nod then grabbed my hand again and proceeded to pull me back through the house, retracing our steps, but instead of climbing the stairs to the upper level of the house, he guided me into a huge room.

It was a lounge but the sheer size of it was overwhelming. The furniture and décor was dark, blacks and greys covering the walls whilst numerous smoked glass fixtures did nothing to break the deep slate shade of the four couches positioned on each wall.

"Wow," I breathed out. "I guess you like gloomy then."

"You'll soon find out there's nothing bright about this room, lamb." I frowned at his cryptic reply. I had long since given up trying to figure out his riddled conversation.

He dropped my hand and tilted his chin towards one of the sofas, ordering me to sit before he stalked harshly across the room. He snatched up two crystal tumblers then returned to me. Staring at the bottle in his hand, he settled beside me then unscrewed the lid.

He brought his nose to rest against the top and inhaled deeply. His eyes closed, his eyelids slowly veiling his delicious muddy gaze as a sigh rattled through him, his senses shivering in ecstasy. I chose to ignore the pulse between my legs as I observed my

Master's eyes roll in delight. It was evidently a favourite brand of his.

He frowned and grumbled something under his breath when he observed me sitting precariously on the edge of the couch, both of my palms tucked securely between my thighs, my back ramrod straight and my eyes flicking over every dark corner of the room. "For Christ's sake, Mae, nothing is going to jump out and devour you."

I flicked my eyes his way. My brow quirked, in return granting me a lift of one of his own. "For pity's sake, drink," he mumbled as he shoved the half full glass of liquor in my hand.

My lips twitched at his frustration. He was a stern, controlled man but my attitude flicked something inside him every time. I could rile him so easily. A small chuckle came from my lips.

He settled back against the cushions and eyed me with suspicion. "Care to share?"

I took a gulp of my own sour whisky. The burn in my throat felt good and I shivered when it flowed into my tummy and heated the chill. "Nothing, really. It just stuns me how much I affect you."

His eyes narrowed into tiny slits. "Your meaning?"

I rested back, imitating his pose as I studied him. He really was spectacular but his handsome features were ruined by his cruel character, his deep rich bronze skin marred by the blackness inside him, and the cold light behind his eyes destroyed his soft gaze. "I can always guarantee that whatever I say or do upsets you. Yet, you still find me humorous and quirky." His eyes widened at my perception. "You desire me, yet hate yourself and deny yourself for that."

"What the…"

I held up a hand. Taking the bull by the horns I continued before he could stop me. "I intrigue you. You can't understand me and that aggravates you, infuriates you even. Whatever or however you try, you know deep down that you will never own me. You will never control me and I will never surrender to your darkness."

"I think you may have underestimated me, Mae."

I shrugged nonchalantly. "Maybe, but what are a few beatings, Master? Your fists will never reach my mind, your harsh cruelty will never brush against my soul. You hate me for that, but you also admire me for it."

He looked furious, my brazenness burning something inside him. Because he knew it was true.

I took another long swallow of my drink. His chest heaved, the cotton of his shirt lifting as he pierced me with the sharpness of his stare. I shrugged again; I had nothing to lose anymore. Although I knew he could rain pain on my body, my frame was fragile enough to snap under it, ending this debilitating wait for death. My mind was secure enough. Fuck his mind games and his attempts to take my sanity. It would never belong to him, and I would never let go of it for him. I was me. I was Mae fucking Swift, daughter of Madeline Swift and Graham Swift, and sister of the strongest fucking heart that had ever graced this God damned diseased planet.

"I won't lie to you, Master. I'm sure you wouldn't want that. On the other hand I won't give you the truths of my life either, nor will you ever be granted my secrets." I held his gaze and smirked. "You want to kill me right now. Please do, nothing would bring me greater delight. I no longer want to be here. That is where you made your first mistake with me." I leaned towards him, the alcohol stripping my anxiety, making me forthright and truthful. "You can't kill someone who is already dead inside."

He exhaled then took a long pull of his drink, his eyes still on mine over the rim of his glass. He moved the glass from his mouth, a twist of his lips on show before he leaned towards the small table before us and gently placed it down.

"You got all that, Mae?"

My stomach shifted as I watched the darkness snake across his deep brown eyes, the tell-tale sign of his cruelty hanging on the very edge of his control.

He nodded slowly and pursed his lips. "I never realised just how perceptive you really are. However, there was one thing you got wrong."

I stared at him. I strived to keep my fear buried, he fed on it, thrived on it and I refused to let him have it.

He slid across the sofa until his thigh pushed against my own, virtually squashing my tiny frame between his large one and the arm of the couch. "The part where you said that I desire you, yet deny myself."

I inched back, the groove of my spine crushing against the wood under the plush fabric. My heart sped up, shifting my pulse into panic mode. Why couldn't I ever shut the hell up? Why the hell had I been made this way, uncontrollable and unruly?

His stare was smouldering, burning a route straight from my eyes into my lower belly.

"Don't!" I snapped. He knew what he was doing, twisting my thoughts with lust, structuring arousal from my fear. "I won't let you."

He barked out a laugh as he took a strand of my hair between his fingers. I jerked back as I attempted to remove myself from danger. However his contact was delicate, the tips of his fingers smoothing my hair between them. He slid his fingers down, gently brushing my scar and along my neck until the full width of his hand spread over my throat.

I gasped and stiffened beneath him, my heart pounding in my ears. Maybe I had underestimated him. He scared me intensely, but I would never let him see that.

His eyes darkened to slate, the intensity of his wrath as potent as his grip on my neck, his fingers slowly blocking the tight tunnel of my lifeline. "I will break you, Mae," he hissed in my ear, his hot breath torture against my cold, damp skin. "I will possess you so entirely that you will ask for permission to fucking breathe."

He stared at me as I stared back, both of us unwilling to back down, both as strong as each other. Courage and determination came from nowhere as my gut bubbled angrily and my mind blocked him, refusing his request for surrender.

"Never," I whispered through the strength of his hold. "I will never be your possession. And I can promise that whatever you do, you will never succeed in breaking me. Only God can break me now and that decision is in his hands."

He held my gaze but his anger was suddenly overwritten by something else and he pulled back, dropping his tight grip on my neck before he picked up his glass and refilled it.

I nodded when he held up the bottle to me in question. "So, Mae Swift," he started as though the previous conversation had been nothing but general gossip, "tell me, what happened to your parents?" He noticed my flinch and looked at me curiously. "Their death still saddens you?"

"Of course it does." Was he for real? "Tell me, Master. Do you have family?"

"We aren't here to discuss my parentage, lamb. I asked you a question."

"And if I choose not to answer?"

He snorted and devoured his drink, the amusement in his eyes bright and clear. "Would you care to find out?"

The edges of my lips lifted involuntary. "You amuse me as much as I amuse you."

"I amuse you?"

I nodded. "Yeah, your dialect, your accent. It makes our conversations quite entertaining."

His top teeth sank into his bottom lip as he tried desperately to hide his reaction to me. I nudged him with my elbow, endeavouring to find the human side of him, the part of him that could interact with me in normal banter.

"Oh come on," I practically pleaded as he stared at me, his gaze far from angry, apprehensive maybe. "There's just us here. For one hour, just us; chat, drink, get insanely drunk, sing rude bloody songs…" I swallowed when he showed no reaction to my request. "Please."

"Why?"

"Because I want to get drunk and have some fun one final time before I die."

I didn't miss the fire that slid across his face, but he managed to bate his anger. He sucked air through his teeth and narrowed his eyes. He seemed to be struggling with his thoughts, the decisions giving him a dilemma he couldn't seem to work out.

"Can I trust you, Mae?"

"Absolutely not."

His face lit up instantly before he snorted and nodded. "Go put on something pretty and meet me here within an hour."

My heart slammed violently against my chest. My brain struggled to work out what he had just said. "Sorry?"

"You want to get drunk, you want to sing your heart out, then we go out. We don't do it here." He leaned towards me causing the hairs on my stubborn body to reach for him. "There are cameras here. You need to relax and get raging drunk without any comeback on either of us. But I need you to promise me, Mae, you give me your word that you will remain by my side constantly." I nodded eagerly, giving him my best smile, the hugest smile I could muster.

"I need to make you aware that the consequences will be dire should you choose to ignore my warning."

"I promise." I knew he meant every word. I knew that so far I hadn't witnessed the extent of his wrath and if I was truthful, I never wanted to witness it.

He stiffened when I leant into him and placed a small kiss on his cheek. "Thank you."

He gulped but nodded. "Go, hurry."

I didn't need to be told twice.

Chapter Fourteen

'Remember there **is** always a price for happine**ss**.'

I laughed at his attempt to dance with me. I had finally found something this arrogant bastard was crap at – dancing.

He smirked, rolling his hips unnaturally as his eyes danced over my own moving body. I shook my head and laughed loudly. "Do not give up your day job," I shouted to him over the loud throb of the tune powering around us. "Maybe next time you should kidnap a dance instructor."

He stared at me, his eyes wide with my sick humour but I shrugged and winked.

"Bloody hell, Mae."

I giggled and danced around his body until I was positioned behind him. Taking his hips in my hands I pushed my front against him and tried to direct his movements, swaying us both to the beat of the music. He placed his own hands over mine and looked behind him to watch what our hips were doing.

"Relax your body," I encouraged. "Close your eyes."

"Uhh."

I rolled my eyes. "I'm not going to run off, you can keep your hands on mine."

He shrugged then did as I asked, closing his eyes and trusting me. I'm not sure what emotion his trust in me evoked but I didn't like the thrum in my chest as I studied his relaxed face, his whole body loosening with the interruption of his sight, his surrender to me quite overwhelming.

I swallowed it back and settled my chin on his shoulder so he could hear me. "Feel the beat, Master." I tapped the side of his hip in tune with the heavy beat of the song. He conformed to my instruction, listening and obeying to what I was telling him. "Let it take over. Allow your body to absorb it."

His body relaxed further against mine, his hips finally moving fluidly. "That's it. A lot better."

He smiled. It was a carefree smile, his entire face untroubled as he concentrated on his body and the beat controlling him. His troubles and concerns evaporated around us when he succumbed to the music and allowed it to take him. His backside pressed against my lower stomach, the firm muscles of his buttocks causing me to briefly forget what I was actually trying to do. The way he ground back against me generated a deep heat to form between my legs. My breathing deepened and I closed my own eyes, letting the moment dictate us both, the sultry rhythm influencing my manipulation while I let myself go for the very last time.

I opened my eyes and blinked when Master turned in my arms until he was facing me. His body still moved with mine, but now it was no longer his backside pressing against me, it was his erection.

He smirked at me when my eyes widened. "You dance skilfully, lamb."

"I had lessons as a child."

He smiled softly. "And what else did your childhood contain?"

"Just the usual stuff. Horse riding lessons, piano lessons and extra maths tutoring. Stuff like that."

"Did you enjoy those particular lessons? It sounds like your childhood was ruled by many different classes and dictations."

"Not at all. My parents appreciated the many opportunities open to Connie and myself. I happen to be grateful for the many possibilities they encouraged."

He watched me, his eyes soft but intense. "You were close to your sister?"

Just the mention of my beautiful sister ached something deep within me. "Yes, we were very close."

"That would be due to the fact she was your twin?"

I blinked at his knowledge, anxiety curling in my stomach when I wondered what else he was privy to. "I suppose, but we were complete opposites. I think that's why we got on so well."

He nodded and smiled, sliding his hands across my lower back to pull me further in. I put it down to the rise in the music volume, making it difficult for him to hear my answers. I had drank quite a few cocktails which had loosened my tongue along with my inhibitions. This was to be a last for me and I both needed and wanted to enjoy it.

"I gather you were the outgoing one." He laughed. I jumped as his hand slid over my bottom, his fingers resting against one arse cheek.

"However did you guess that?"

He shook his head and smiled but then his smile disappeared. "You must miss her."

"I do, very much. I lost half of myself when…"

When I didn't finish my sentence he nodded, as if aware of the pain inside me when I spoke of her. I wasn't sure how much he knew of Connie's death. I didn't want him to know if he didn't already.

Our bodies still moved to the music as Master spun us round, his hands now moving round to hold my hips the way I had held his. "Mae…"

I lifted my eyes to his when his words seemed to get stuck in his throat.

"It's okay. Ask."

Wariness crossed his handsome face, darkening his eyes as he studied me intently. I knew he was trying to read my mood as the conversation steered into dangerous ground. "I take it Connie was very close to your father."

His statement told me exactly how much information he had gained, the rest of it I wasn't so sure. "How much do you know?"

He held my eyes, showing me that he had no guilt over the knowledge. "A little. The reason she took her own life I mainly guessed, but it's quite common knowledge that it was due to the fact she lost herself with the death of your father."

I nodded sadly, tears pricking my eyes as my past once more found a way to hurt me. "Yes." It was all I could answer with but he already knew there was nothing more I could tell him.

"You refrained from following her. Were you never tempted to take the route your family took?"

"My parents didn't die on purpose," I snapped.

"I know, Mae. Calm down, I'm just asking if you ever wanted to take your own life like your sister did. That is all."

I locked eyes with him, making him see me as I answered him honestly. "All the damn time. I tried many times but I'm Mae Swift, I struggle to even do that right. Many bodge jobs brought on the wrath of social services and numerous therapists. You have no idea how many times I tried to take the same way out as Connie, yet here I am. Waiting for the end with you."

He narrowed his eyes, his pupils darkening to onyx, the heat behind them blazing. "You need to understand that when the time comes, you won't be with me, Mae. You will be in the care of your new Master."

"What?" I reared back causing his hands to drop from me. "How soon?"

He didn't answer as he took hold of my hand and led me back over to our booth in the corner. He nodded to the waitress to bring us more drinks before he urged me into the seat and slid in beside me, trapping me securely between him and the wall.

He turned in the seat to face me. "A month. It all depends on how your progression goes."

"Progression? What progression?"

He sighed, pausing when the waitress brought our refills. "I have absolutely no idea why I'm telling you this, lamb." He hesitated and for a moment and I thought he might have changed his mind about being open but he carried on. "You and other stock are due for auction before six weeks' time."

I swallowed back the nausea that threatened to make a fool out of me in the middle of the club. "Other stock?"

"Yes, I told you before; there are others under my guidance."

I stared at him, gauging his mood and weighing up how far I could go with him. "Are the… others in the house with us?"

He blinked at me, his eyes fixed intensely on me so he could read me. I had nothing to hide, he could interpret my reactions whichever way he wanted to. "Just one other. I only take on two per course."

"Course?"

He nodded. "Yes. That's what I do in a certain way. Provide education to subjects that are somewhat… taboo."

"You teach slavery."

He smiled wickedly, his eyes glistening in the many different coloured lights bouncing around us. "In a way but I prefer to call it 'pain acceptance'."

"What the…" I ran my tongue over the inside of my cheek to put a stop on the flurry of swear words that were threatening to erupt. I leaned forward, shuffling my bottom round so I could face him. "Forgive me for being so… inquisitive, Master but…"

He nodded when I paused and bit into my lip. I wanted the answers to so many questions but I was also wary of how he would interpret my probing. "Go on. We're here not as teacher and pupil. I've brought you because it was your request. Although you think I'm a monster, Mae, you may also not be aware that monsters have hearts like the rest of the animals on this planet."

I stared at him. "So you admit you're a monster?"

He laughed loudly, his whole face lighting up. "I've never denied the fact, my darling."

His endearment seemed to slither around me until it crept into my heart forbiddingly. I shouldn't allow him to use his manipulation, because of course that's all it was. But the way he was, the way his own unique personality demanded that I pay attention didn't allow me to do anything else but let him inside.

"I always thought monsters didn't possess empathy."

His eyes narrowed when he caught the bitter tone in my voice. "And just how many monsters have you come across, Mae?"

"I'm quite sure more than you have."

"And you know that for a fact do you? You never question or inquire of other people's lives. You just assume, Mae Swift and that is where you make your first downfall. You should never presume but always read the truths from the lies."

"Your lies drown the truth, Master. How do you expect me to decipher between the two?"

He leaned even further until his face was directly in front of mine, the alcohol on his breath mixing with my own as we created our own unique cocktail of air. "I have never lied to you." His truth hit me forcefully. He was correct, he had never lied to me but that still didn't make him an honest person; far from it. "If anyone here is untruthful then that would be you, lamb. You are never honest with yourself, never mind with me."

"Really?" I downed my fresh drink, savouring the heat that hit my belly and the fluffiness that curled around my brain. I'd had far too many drinks and in the company that I had, I knew it could be a dangerous thing. "And where are my dishonesties, Master? I can't recall lying to you."

He watched me for a while, his face impassive but his eyes suddenly sad and painful. "You tell me you're not scared of death, Mae. That you are waiting expectantly for it. But I see the truth, I see how very scared you are, how you wish life had been different. You won't accept this life you were given. You blame God, others, maybe even your parents for how your life has turned out."

"You arrogant bas..." I took a calming breath when his face darkened with my outburst and turned to him angrily. "You know nothing about me, Master. If you did, you would know that right at the moment death takes me I will be applauding along with every other damn person on this planet."

I flinched when his palm slid over my cheek. I didn't realise a tear had fallen until he wiped it away with his thumb. He removed his hand and looked down at his fingers as he gently slid the drop between his thumb and forefinger. "You see, lamb. This little drop of your pain tells me that although it's singular, it's very potent. It contains every single ounce of despair that is churning up inside you. It tells me you fight against the pain when you should be accepting it and letting other tears follow. Holding onto grief is suicide. It never soothes, it tears you apart until you become twisted, morphed into a slice of horror that even the devil would refuse to condone."

"No." Grieving helped nothing but pain, the only thing it helped was self-pity and heartache and I for one would stubbornly refuse to allow it to overrule me.

He sighed and shook his head. "Great night out, lamb. You are the life of the party."

My eyes widened on him before the laughter burst from my mouth. "Well, you're just the perfect date, Master. You haven't even fed me." I nudged him with my elbow and winked, grateful for his change of conversation.

He slapped his hand on his chest and smiled widely. "Well forgive me, my darling. How very rude of me. What would you like?"

I giggled and smirked at him. "Do you know what I really fancy?" He quirked an eyebrow. "Chips with tons and tons of salt and vinegar to eat on the walk back to your house."

"My house?"

"Yeah, why are we going somewhere else?"

He leaned back in the seat and smiled at me. "No. If you had the choice of going anywhere before you die, where would you like to go?"

"That's easy." I smiled sadly, pulling in a fortifying breath as I stared at the remainder of pink liquid in the bottom of my glass. "The beach."

"Any beach?" His stare triggered goose bumps to flare over my skin. It was too searching, his desire to see inside of me simply terrifying. There was only ever me that knew what happened inside my head and I refused to let anyone else see that part of me.

"Yes. It was just something I always did with my parents and Connie. We would visit the beach regularly." I shrugged as heat flamed my cheeks. "It's just me, something…"

"I understand." His smile was soft but it gave away another side of him, one I thought he didn't possess. "Come on." He slid out of the booth and held out his hand for me. "Let's fill that belly with greasy chips."

"You don't like chips?" I asked as I placed my hand in his.

"No. I find them too heavy."

I rolled my eyes at him, laughing. "Have you ever lived? You're way too serious."

We crossed the dance floor as we made our way out of the building. Just as I was about to step off the wooden floor, a random man took hold of my waist and swung me around to him. He smiled widely as he started to press against me and sway in time to the music. My hand dropped from Master's as he pulled me further against him.

He smiled widely as the loud music and atmosphere in the room manipulated us. The Jackson's, *Can You Feel It* played deafeningly around us, the beat in the song enlivening the part of me that wanted to dance. His grip on my hips was strong as he forced me around until his groin pressed against my lower back.

"I love this song," he shouted in my ear. "Move with me, baby."

I laughed and let it flow. It was good to dance with someone who owned the music as I did, another person feeling the beat in his soul.

The whole of the floor moved with us, every single person feeling the song take over as we all moved with the DJ, The Jackson's demanding that we give in to their brilliant ability to own you with music.

I stumbled slightly as I leant back and my dance partner disappeared. However, just as I was about to turn around, different large hands slid around me until I was pulled back into a firm wall of muscle. Fingers splayed over the slight roundness of my tummy, a strong chest supported the weight of my back and a large erection pulsed against my bottom.

I hated the way my body reacted instantly to him, the throb in my lower belly matching the pulse in my pussy. My chest heaved as my nipples hardened with need and blood surged into my brain making me lightheaded and woozy.

"Your body demands to be owned, lamb. The way it moves claims every man's attention in this room." The way his hot breath whispered over my ear made me wonder what it would feel like to have his mouth between my thighs, how it would empower me to have him taste my pleasure.

"There's something wrong with me."

I didn't realise I had openly voiced the statement until Master spoke quietly in my ear. "Because you desire me?"

"Yes." It was a whisper but an honest whisper. "I hate the way you manipulate me, Master. It confuses me, makes my mind argue with my body."

I closed my eyes and groaned when he started to grind his heavy cock into the crease of my arse, the thin dress I had chosen to wear providing little barrier between us. "Oh, God."

His breathing deepened, the current of hot air over my ear heavier but slower. His hands made their way upwards until they were spread over my ribs. His hold on me was tight, entrapping me between his body and his hands. I felt like his possession, his property, but what frightened me more was his ability to make me feel there was no one else in the room with us, just him and me. My body betrayed me, causing a horrific confliction between sensation and reality.

I was his hostage, his plaything, yet suddenly and somewhat insanely I wanted to be his toy, the pawn in his sick game. I wanted to be controlled and used to his satisfaction. I wanted him to take me and mould me into something he wanted me to be. I needed him to put a stop to this need in me but I also wanted him to encourage the dark side of me. I had never been so at odds with different sides of me as I was then.

I turned in his arms. "Why do you do this to me?" I needed to see the truth in his answer as well as feel it.

"I do nothing, Mae. Your reaction is all you, my darling. It's the part of you that is hidden, another of your lies that you refuse to accept. You crave this darkness. I knew as soon as I saw your reaction to the situation I put you in that it was locked deep inside you. I just so happen to possess the key that has unlocked the kink inside you."

"There is no *kink* inside me. I choose to think it's inexperience. How you could ever think that I condone this situation you have thrust upon me is beyond me."

We still moved to the music, our bodies locked together, twisted into one moving entity. "I'm not saying you condone it. However answer me one question truthfully and then I'll let this... this *connection* between us go."

I stared at him, worried about what his question would be, but I eventually nodded. I promised myself to answer as truthfully as I could, more for my benefit than his. I needed to understand the part of me that he awoke.

"How arousing is pain?"

I swallowed, dropping my gaze from his. The answer was already formed in my head. It was already something I often subconsciously asked myself. He was just the one to actually voice the question.

"Be honest with yourself, not just me. Accept that part of you, Mae. But let me make one thing clear. I can bring that side of you to life. I have the ability to pull out your desire and free it from you. I am the very person who can allow you to find comfort in the one thing you need, give you the light you crave from the dark."

"I don't..."

"Don't lie to yourself, lamb." His eyes were hard as one of his hands spread across the nape of my neck and the other slid into my hair, his fingers twisting the roots into his fist, making me gasp. I chose to ignore the deep throb that developed inside me. He didn't speak for the longest time, just kept me in his harsh grip and pierced me with those damn hypnotising eyes.

"I don't understand how you can have this effect on me when I hate you." I was as honest as I could be but also anxious at how he would react to my straightforwardness.

He smiled slightly giving me a reprieve over the worry I held. "You don't have to like somebody for them to arouse you, lamb. Your reaction to me is just how nature intended us to procreate."

"The way I feel about you is far from natural."

He smirked. "Let's experiment shall we?"

"What exactly do you have in mind?"

He shook his head and took hold of my hand once again. "Not yet, lamb. First we go get you some of those chips you desire."

I allowed him to lead me out. I was too nervous to refuse his possessive hold. He seemed to seethe at anyone who looked at me or stood in my path as they silently asked me to dance with them. I frowned at them all; my scar usually scared them off.

"They're not repulsed by me," I stated as Master tilted his head questioningly when he saw my confused look.

"Why would they be repulsed by you?"

"My scar."

He rolled his eyes in frustration. "I've told you, it's only you who sees it as it is. You are still you, Mae. People in this room just see another partier, another much like themselves who likes to let go to the music for a while."

"No," I answered over the music. "I can promise not all people are like that."

"If you're referring to the scum on your estate, then I can tell you honestly that they only see what their personalities want them to see. They see the sadness inside you and react to it, therefore boosting their own confidence with your anxiety."

"How do you know how I'm treated at home?"

We managed to push through the door and onto the street before any more revellers stopped us. The cold wind bit at me, generating a deep shudder through me. Master pulled me closer to him. "I told you. You have been on my radar for three years. I make it my business to know about you, especially as you were chosen for education."

"Chosen?"

He flicked a glance my way and sighed irritably. "Enough!"

My footing stuttered as I came to an abrupt stop, angered by his sudden barked order. "What? I think I deserve an explanation to why this is all happening. Who chose me? Was it you? Did I fit the bill as to what kind of human being you like to twist and morph into something your sick desires want?"

I had been *chosen.* How the hell he hadn't expected my anger by that notion I had no idea.

He dropped my hand and stormed ahead but my stubborn side refused to allow him to hide from me. I scurried beside him, my heels clacking loudly on the pavement in my haste to keep up with him. His strong wide steps were as furious as he was, anger rolling off him as each foot thudded loudly on the concrete.

"Come on, Master. I deserve an explanation."

People were starting to stare at us, me chasing after a huge guy, furiously barking questions at him as he chose to ignore me and just concentrate on his rage. I should have noticed the wrath simmering beneath his calm exterior. Maybe I did, but I refused to allow it to scare me out of pursuing answers. I deserved them, it was my life after all, and I needed to understand why I no longer owned myself or had a choice in how the rest of it would be played out.

"Answer me, damn you. Who the hell chose me? It wasn't you, was it?"

His fingers dug into my upper arm as he dragged me down an alley, darkness and shadows seeping deeper around us the further down the alley we went. I didn't see the danger; my fury was too intense to see anything else.

"You tell me, Daniel. TELL ME!"

His hand covered my mouth, cutting off my words and my oxygen supply as he slid his palm over my mouth and my nose.

"I suggest you calm down, lamb. I am so close to cutting your throat right now, but if I'm honest, the only reason I won't is because a clean-up down an alley would be somewhat irritating."

My back hit the brick wall behind me with a thud. I struggled beneath him, anger still controlling my stupidity. My lungs squeezed tight as they fought for air but every single inch of me fumed with his inability to answer my question.

My heart rate pounded in my ears, the thump almost hypnotising as life drained from me quickly.

I implored with my eyes, begging him to let me go and allow me much needed air. He narrowed his eyes, enjoyment heavy in his expression as he once more overpowered me and took God's place, deciding whether to let me live or die.

My fist slammed into his chest as I struggled to breathe beneath his hand. My legs started to tremble as my vision tunnelled and a whooshing sound echoed in my ears. He sneered at me, the curl of his lips mocking and cruel until he suddenly moved back.

I gulped at the instant availability of air, my mouth opening and closing like a damn guppy's. My chest heaved painfully as my lungs powered back to life.

"Why do you do that?" I shouted. "Every damn time I upset you, you try to suffocate me. What the hell is wrong with you? I only asked a bloody question."

He stepped into me but I didn't notice his proximity as I still fought to bring back consciousness. Everything hummed around me as my brain struggled to cope with the sudden rush of oxygen.

I gasped when his body pushed against mine and the groove of each brick indented its shape into my spine. His furious eyes held me, overpowered me. "You never, ever use my name again."

I blinked at him. "After all that, that's all you focus on? You try and kill me, yet all you're bothered about is that I called you Daniel?"

I was angry, confused, stunned; every emotion possible coursing through me with a speed I couldn't keep up with. I stared as hard as he did, denying him my surrender and refusing to show him any weakness.

"Believe me, little lamb, if I wanted to kill you then you wouldn't be stood there arguing like the stubborn woman you are."

"What the hell is your problem with me? I can't do this anymore. You have more sides than a Rubix Cube, each a different colour, a different mood. How do you expect me to surrender to you when I find it impossible to understand you? I never know what is expected of me, I never know how to treat you. I don't even know what the hell I feel anymore. You confuse me, anger me, humour me... heal me."

Tears pricked my eyes, burning my sight as much as they burnt my heart. My mind was shattering into various parts, each an assortment of different thoughts as my brain struggled to decipher each one.

He was silhouetted in the moonlight, each contour of his handsome face highlighted eerily until he resembled something ethereal and ghostly.

He dropped his forehead, his brow slotting against mine as we both fought with the commotion in our heads.

"You intrigue me, Mae Swift. You make me question myself." His honesty grounded me. It took hold of something inside me and twisted it until all I could feel was guilt, his manipulation once more muddling everything.

"Please don't use this to hurt me." I whispered the words but my soul shouted them. I needed some sort of stability, something real I could take hold of. "Answer me one question truthfully."

He regarded me for a while but when he nodded I plunged ahead before he changed his mind. "Do you… have you ever… regretted what you do to women?"

His eyes widened as though he had expected some other query. "Honestly, please," I begged.

He swallowed heavily as his gaze locked with mine to show me the truth in his answer. "Not until now. I've watched you, Mae. Watched you struggle with life, and for some insane moments, I actually wanted to give you a smile. I've never felt that before, the want to please. You confuse me, make everything I know… knew, for once seem wrong and…"

"And?"

"And…" He gulped and ran the tip of his nose down the length of mine. My body shivered as something other than arousal caused the blood in my veins to flow freer. "Every year I came to you, you never changed. You still held a deep sadness. The first year you were beyond approach. You hid away in that dark, dismal home of yours and I barely caught a glimpse of you. I initially thought you had died and for the first time in my life I felt something other than the need to hurt and cause pain. I wanted to check you were okay and that confused the hell out of me. You hide from me and for the first time in my life I need to see all of you, feel all of you."

My heart bled with his words. Memories stabbed my soul once more. A tear freed itself and rolled down my cheek, the taste of it bitter when it trickled onto my lips.

My hand lifted to his face warily, my palm cupping his cheek. "I'm glad you only visited me at Christmas, there are some things that... that are too hurtful to share with you. From the day you took my soul, you never left me. You lived inside me, more than you may think. You refused to leave my nightmares, your hurtful words and cruel taunts lived my life for me. I couldn't push them away, you brought me down further than my parents' and Connie's death ever could."

He swallowed, his eyes soaking up my words. "But you came back, refusing me any peace before I get to leave. My secrets will go with me, Master. They need to go with me. Please don't push them from me, I will never forgive myself if..." Noise down the alley made us both jump, pulling us from our moment of honesty and connection.

"We need to go," he said. He turned to take my hand once more. "I will not let you go until I know everything you're hiding from me, lamb. I'm sorry if that grieves you, but you will make your peace before you leave. Whether it be with me, God or even yourself, those secrets will no longer be mysteries to the world before you leave it."

I begged to differ.

Chapter Fifteen

'Limits are limitless when you strive
for more.'

Master grabbed my hand and pulled me out of the taxi. The fresh air had intensified my drunkenness, taking my stability and exchanging it for unsteadiness, the world beneath my feet as tilted as my posture. His arm slid around my waist when I swayed and bumped into the cab door. He rolled his eyes at the driver as he shoved some money at him. "Excuse my girlfriend's attempts to destroy your car. Any damage, you can find me here at this address."

The driver smiled and waved him off. "Don't worry, mate. It's dealt with more than a body or two denting the door."

Master nodded and took hold of me, shutting the door with his hip as he led me towards the house. "How much have I allowed you to drink?"

I giggled as I fell up the first step. "You make a useless guide dog."

He shook his head but chuckled as he slid the key in the door and it swung open. "I'm so thirsty," I told him as I licked at the salt still lingering on my lips from the chips I'd greedily devoured. "I need a nice white wine spritzer. You know how to make them, Master?"

He didn't answer. The door handle jabbed my hip as I tried to manoeuvre myself through the door and I turned to scowl at it; damn thing should have moved out of my way. "Maybe we could try different wines to make our own concoction. You have enough varieties down in your cellar to..."

I slammed to a halt when I witnessed our welcome committee. Master stood rigid before me but I didn't miss how he shifted in front of me, shielding me from whoever had come to greet us.

The Demi-whore was stood with a smirk on her face, Frank beside her; great worry on his soft face as his eyes found mine. I waved to him, grinning at the sight of his calming features. "Hey Frank, you missed a great night out. Next time you must come with us."

He frowned, his head shaking slightly from side to side as though warning me of something. His gaze flicked to the man next to him before he lowered his eyes. I turned to look at whomever Frank wanted me to see. He was a big bloke, his huge muscles contained in an expensive charcoal suit. His face was as dark as his attire, the deep rich chocolate of his eyes as familiar as the structure of his strong chin.

"Hi," I greeted as I stepped from behind Master. "I'm Mae."

He didn't move, his body locked as his hands clasped tightly in front of him. He slid his stern stare from Master to me. "I know who you are. I'm presuming you have no idea who I am?"

His dialect and accent was the exact same as Master's and I frowned, pursing my lips as I studied him. "I'm gathering you're a relation of Master's."

Master stiffened but remained silent. Tension rolled from him in waves but I couldn't understand why. The man took a step towards us, his eyes still fixed on me. "Nadu!" He suddenly barked.

Instinct sent a potent warning through me. I couldn't say what it was but I knew it was important that I follow orders from this man, for Master's sake as much as my own.

I dropped into position beside Master, taking comfort from his proximity as fear drowned out the alcohol in my system and filled me with dread. He relaxed slightly at my obedience. I slackened further when he placed his hand gently on top of my head. "Good girl," he whispered tightly. I didn't acknowledge his praise. I remained still as was expected of me, my chin high but my eyes on nothing specific.

The older man circled around me, his steps rhythmic and heavy, hypnotising me. Master's thumb stroked slowly across the crown of my head, soothing as well as supporting me. Something was off. Master's apprehension, Demi's delight, Frank's anguish were all notifying me that I needed to behave for once.

"Tell me," the man addressed me. "I'm intrigued. Where did your outing tonight take you?"

Oh shit. I knew instantly that we were in trouble. Panic rushed through me causing my heart rate to speed up as my stomach twisted with anguish. "Uhh..."

I yelped when his fingers gripped my hair. He stood behind me, his body close. His anger suffocated me, filling every fibre of me with fear as his supremacy ruled over everyone in the room. Master stepped to the side but I caught the tightening of his fist from the corner of my eye. "Father..." he attempted but the large man ignored him, bending into me until his mouth was beside my ear.

"Answer my question!"

"It was my fault, sir. I..." I cried out as his grip hardened, the pull on my roots burning my scalp as he yanked me upright. My hands instinctively rose to his, my fingers wrapping around his as I attempted to loosen his hold.

"Do not insult me with your lies, girl."

"I'm not. I asked to get drunk one last time before I... before I die."

He scoffed and started to drag me across the room. "Meet me in your office in one hour," he spoke to Master without looking his way.

"Father, this has nothing to do with Mae. It was my decision."

"Do you not think I already know that, boy? Your subject needs to know her place. I will deal with you after I have instilled some discipline into her. You both need to accept the consequences of your actions."

What the hell was wrong with this guy? "We didn't do anything wrong. I didn't leave Master's side. I ... Christ!" I squealed when he tugged harder on my hair. "If I'd have wanted to lose my hair I would have undergone chemo!"

"MAE!" Master barked, chastising me for my rudeness.

"Do not worry, Daniel. I'll teach her some manners." The certainty with which he spoke filled me with fear. I had no doubt he would stick to his promise.

I suddenly knew who had given the order for my auction. Master's father managed the business, if one could call it a business. I was also aware of some deep control issues between father and son. However their relationship was the least of my worries. I was more concerned how far this man would take my punishment. It wasn't difficult to presume he was far fiercer than his son, the way he dragged me through the house told me how self-important he was, how much he demanded respect and how he considered himself superior to anyone else.

"Demi," Master's father spoke kindly to the very person who didn't deserve any respect. "Please prepare Lola for indulgence, but before that I require her presence to witness what her rival's behaviour brings."

Lola? Rival? I wasn't aware of any rivalry going on. I knew there was another in the same situation as me, but rivals? I wouldn't have exactly described us as that, more like allies who had both been thrust into a horrific nightmare.

My eyes caught Master's before I was pulled through a door. His expression was of apprehension but mostly guilt. I didn't understand the reason for that; it was my fault. Even though Master had made the suggestion, I knew it was because of our connection that he had relented and tried to give me something 'normal' before I died. His compassion had turned into punishment. But I needed to take it, if only for his sake.

It was this thought, that I was willing to take punishment to save my Master that caused me greater anguish than the reprimand that was coming. I couldn't grasp why I wanted to shield him when he had done nothing but hurt me. The way my thoughts showed more concern for my Master than me worried me.

I did wonder if it was the tumour fogging everything that filled my head, contorting normality into make-believe, taking emotions that should be there and structuring something false in their place.

However, these thoughts didn't last long when my punishment began. Every single thought in my head turned to pain and misery as Master's father showed me exactly why he reigned above his son.

Lola turned out to be a pretty girl with long lustrous blonde hair and deep inquisitive blue eyes; piercing blue eyes that supported me throughout the duration of my Master's father's hour long rapes and beatings.

Lola's sad face kept me going in the worst hour I had ever witnessed. I had thought once that Daniel's rape couldn't ever be matched in darkness but his father showed me just how naive I had been. He demonstrated that however terrible I thought life had become, there was a deeper more intense terror that could be found with each sick and twisted way he took me.

He lapped at my blood whilst he drove pain and torment through my brittle body. His sickening grunts of satisfaction filled me with a misery I had never experienced before in my short twenty one years. He took me with sickening objects, sex toys that belonged in some sick fetish club, as well as himself, and once *as well* as himself, many, many times; some so vile they actually caused me to vomit. But that didn't stop him, he continued to torture with whips, floggers, a long thin crop plugged with barbed metal spikes until I was a wreck. My skin hung loosely from my limp body as my tears stung the numerous cuts and grazes to my face.

Yet, it was his cruel words of disgust and degradation that finally broke my will to live; the humiliating names, the shameful declarations of what he was doing to me and the insults about how useless I was for him. The way he used and abused me was nothing to the way he persecuted my self-belief and destroyed my character.

Each tear that spilled from Lola gave me the courage to hold on to my sanity. Each small smile she managed to give me throughout my ordeal showed me that someone was with me, embracing me spiritually and telling me to hold the fuck on to the end. She refused to let me go all the way through it as she knelt for an hour where she had been told, her strong stare linking with mine and telling me silently that I wasn't alone during my travel through hell.

I held onto her gaze, greedily taking whatever she gave me until the suffering became too much and I sank into the misery my subconscious had waiting for me.

Chapter Sixteen

'Preparing for death does not mean you are ready for it.'

I didn't see Master for many days after our night out. He never came to me in my fevered days of oblivion. I put my state down to the fact that my poorly brain couldn't cope with anymore; and I let it be, allowed it to rest.

I was somewhat aware of Pauline and Frank's presence, sometimes the deep scratch of Dr Galloway's medication pulling me from my frenzied dreams, but it was the fact my subconscious forever hunted for the dark man that had taken my soul that refused me any rest.

I woke after four days to bright sunshine seeping through the window. My room was empty, my breathing the only sound in the room as the serenity of the wall of butterflies soothed the jargon in my mind. Before my vision was granted focus, the soft fluttery wings on each insect appeared to wave and flicker, their morning dance accompanying the deep rich song of the spring birds.

I frowned when one particular butterfly, the bright blue one I forgot the name of, pulled away from the rest and drifted along a ray of sunshine towards me. It landed softly on the very edge of my bed, its gentle black eyes staring at me. Its wings curled around its body, cocooning itself protectively as it considered me for a moment.

We held each other in a gaze of awe and amazement, as though neither of us had ever witnessed the other being before. It shifted slightly, its tiny body vibrating as it attempted to both protect itself but allow me access to its beauty.

Neither of us moved, both of us prisoners to each other and the room. It sympathised with me, I could feel its pity and sorrow. I could sense its promise of paradise, the fantasy of glory forthcoming and I knew its message was from the heavens, giving me guidance for the coming end.

"I'm ready," I whispered, not caring how stupid or strange it seemed. I needed it to deliver my message and bring me the peace I so craved for. I hungered for death now, craved for the oblivion of the end. "Please. Hurry."

"Mae?"

I blinked as the room finally came into focus and Pauline's voice broke the spell of the moment. There was only myself seated on the large bed, the pretty blue butterfly once again housed on the wall next to its neighbours. I stared at it, willing it to move. I needed to know my brain wasn't deteriorating further but it remained still, frozen in its own death as if it hadn't forewarned me of mine.

"How are you feeling?"

I stared at Pauline with bewilderment. She seemed more out of concept than the butterfly had.

"Are you okay? You look a little pale." She bustled over to me, placing the back of her hand on my forehead.

Nothing seemed to work; my mind, my body, my senses, they were all frozen and slack. My mouth wouldn't form words as I stared at her, the only thing that seemed to work was my eyesight.

"Okay, honey," she soothed as she directed me back against the mattress. "I'm going to fetch Dr Galloway. I'll be right back."

I couldn't nod, my brain wouldn't tell my head what to do. My lungs still forced air in and out, my eyes still showed me what the world was up to, my nostrils still told me breakfast was cooking, yet my brain couldn't seem to decipher any of the information these senses were detecting.

I didn't panic. I didn't worry. I was too high on confusion to decode what was happening. The serenity that ran through me calmed any anguish that my sudden disability brought, taking away any fear that death portrayed.

The birds sang even louder as though heralding my journey into heaven, their arousing song stunning and delightful.

I managed a small smile as my eyes slid closed and I welcomed peace.

"She's deteriorating."

Master's voice echoed through my head but my brain still refused to control any muscle or joint in my tired body. Exhaustion was the only thing I felt, although my senses were still aware. I could smell the subtle aroma of Master's scent, his unique trace of citrus and mint mixed with his woody cologne. I could hear each word that was spoken, I could even taste whatever Pauline had cooked up that day but I was trapped inside a frozen body; a useless form, a living corpse.

"Yes, I'm afraid she is." Dr Galloway's voice was filled with compassion and sadness as he replied to Master's words.

"How long does she have?"

The doctor sighed, as though weighing up my life. "I'm not too sure. A week, maybe two."

Silence descended around me as anger controlled my thoughts. I thought the butterfly had told of my plea, that it had come to take me. But now I knew it had just been my tumour playing cruel tricks on my brain.

"Will she remain this way... paralysed?" Master's question caused my heart to speed up. I didn't want to lose the ability to move in the last moments. I had refused treatment because of its debilitating symptoms.

"No. Your father's beating caused her brain to swell. That in itself is putting the tumour under some difficult strain. Once the swelling has subsided she should feel much better. Give her time to rest, Daniel. I'll make her as comfortable as possible."

"Yes."

I tried to frown at the small squeak in Master's voice but of course, I couldn't.

"I..." The doctor paused, deliberating his words. "There's something special about this one?"

A suffocating atmosphere suddenly descended, filling the air with a thickness that my lungs struggled to cope with. "Special?"

"Forgive me if you think I'm being forward Daniel but... I can't understand why you seem to care. She'll be removed from your guidance soon. You educate and sculpt, then send them to the highest bidder, that's how it's always been. But this one seems to have..."

"Enough!"

"I'm being a friend here, not a colleague. Talk to me, Daniel."

"You can leave now." Master was final in his words, the doctor sensed it as much as I did.

"Fine," Dr Galloway sighed. "But be careful, Daniel. Your father will make you both pay for any relationship you develop."

"There is no relationship, Philip. She is just... just the stock that has seen the highest bids."

The doctor scoffed and I could picture him shaking his head. "Sure."

Nothing more was said before the door clicked closed. I was sure I was alone until soft fingers brushed away a strand of hair that was tickling my nose. A physical sadness filled the air when Master sighed heavily. I tried so hard to open my eyes when his thumb stroked the length of my cheekbone and he repeated a sigh.

But then he was gone, quiet once more enveloping me as sleep did the same.

"You look much better." Pauline smiled widely at me as I lifted another spoon of soup to my mouth. I gave her a small smile in return.

I wasn't sure how much more time had passed since I had overheard Master and the doctor's conversation but I hadn't heard or sensed him again after that.

Pauline's soup seemed to have miracle qualities, aiding me and building my strength with every swallow. "This soup is good, Pauline. Do you make it yourself?"

She nodded as she pulled various clothes from the huge wardrobe. "Yes." She smiled proudly. "It was my mother's recipe. Chicken, celery and a secret item."

I laughed with her. "Well it's wonderful. Thank you."

She gave me a pained smile and I narrowed my eyes on her. "What?"

She wrung her fingers furiously and took a deep breath. "Master requires your company with some visitors tonight."

"Oh." I didn't like the swoop of anguish in my stomach. Nerves and anxiety put me off my food and I placed the spoon beside the half-filled bowl. "Will it... will it be like the breakfast?"

She knew I was referring to the pedestal. She swallowed and nodded. "Just do as you are expected and everything will run like clockwork." Her false enthusiasm intensified the anxiety inside me.

"Do I have a choice?"

Her brow puckered, her age instantly showing on her worried face. She didn't answer my question but she didn't have to. We both knew that I definitely didn't have a choice.

She held up a beautiful deep red dress with a hopeful smile. "Look how pretty this is, Mae. You will look stunning."

I nodded faintly. "I suppose there's underwear to match. If you can call it underwear." I knew I would have to wear the bloody half-knickers that were expected last time.

"Yes. And please wear them this time. You could have gotten Master into a lot of trouble if your last ensemble had been witnessed."

I rolled my eyes at her. "Oh we can't have Master getting into trouble, can we?"

She gave me a worried glance, her brow pinched and a slight tightening to her lips. "Please, as much for your benefit as his. Master Robert will be at tonight's celebrations. Don't anger him any further Mae, please."

I presumed Master Robert to be Master's father. I nodded, understanding completely that what he had done to me had probably only been a portion of what he could deliver. I had never met anyone as cruel and twisted as him and I was adamant I didn't want to meet his violent side again.

"Fine."

She smiled widely at me, relief in her eyes. "Come, let's get you ready. I'll make you look pretty."

I huffed as I climbed from the bed. "Yeah, good luck with that."

I stood staring at the door as Pauline flustered around me, her nervous fiddling with sections of my hair irritating me. "Pauline, please, it's fine. In fact it's perfect."

My chest tightened as my stomach clenched with nerves. I couldn't pinpoint why but I knew something big was to happen behind the door to the room where Master and I had shared a bottle of expensive whisky. Call it premonition or just plain instinct, it didn't matter, I just knew deep in my soul that that night would change many things.

The door opened and Master stepped out. The tightness in my chest at the sight of him was both comforting but confusing. His handsome familiarity and strength gave me a sense of protection but the way his stare hardened cautioned me.

"Master?"

He pursed his lips and straightened his spine, both actions intending to remove our new relationship. Whatever had happened whilst I had been out of it had taken away his compassion and replaced it with a deep-seated disgust. The way his cold eyes roved over my body and the small sneer that crafted his mouth made me realise our friendship was over.

I was angry with him but at the same time I understood why. I knew his father had been as cruel to him over his leniency with me as he had been to me. However, I was more upset that he had just dropped our mutual understanding of each other without fighting for what he actually wanted. Or maybe this *was* what he wanted and I had just misread the signals he had given off.

He had admitted that there was something about me that made his usual cruelty veer off towards something warmer. Even if he hadn't understood what it was, I had. So the fact that he had once more allowed the bitterness to consume him and destroy what little hope he'd had of redemption disappointed and hurt me.

He stepped towards me, causing me to stiffen. He narrowed his eyes. I could sense the change in him and I preserved what little dignity I had left by shutting him out as much as he had closed himself off to me.

"It is imperative that you behave tonight, Mae." He turned to Pauline. "Did you make sure she was obedient in my choice of underwear?"

Pauline nodded. "Yes, Master."

He nodded. "Thank you. You may leave." I was surprised Pauline didn't curtsey before she hurried away.

Master turned back to me, his eyes once again studying my figure in the silk red dress he had requested I wore for him. His tongue snaked across his lips, dampening them as his gaze dropped to look at my tiny feet slotted into the ridiculously high red heels.

He tipped his head as he lifted his eyes back to my face. "You look very beautiful. Thank you for your cooperation tonight."

I snorted loudly and shook my head. "Cooperation, Master? I think we both know it is nothing to do with cooperation. Cooperation suggests that you allow yourself to aid the person that needs help. And come on, whether or not I want to assist, you demand it of me."

He glowered at me, his chest heaving in anger. His fingers gripped my chin, bruising my tender jaw under his punishing hold. "Not tonight, Mae. I will not stand for your rebellion."

I locked my jaw defiantly, silently telling him that whatever pain he inflicted, I would take it and refuse to let it destroy me. "Oh you needn't worry, Master. I gather my buyer is here tonight and the last thing I would want to do is put him off. The last thing we both want is to be stuck with each other."

His eyes widened at my outburst but his fingers dug into my cheeks so he could pull my face close. The spiteful smirk on his face made my heart thud precariously. "I wouldn't worry about that too much, lamb. The loser doesn't get to stay behind either."

The way he said it, full of unspoken promise, surged dread through every single fibre of me. "What do you mean? What happens to the loser?"

He barked out a tight laugh. "Tell me, Mae. What happens to other pawns in a game when they don't make it to the end square?"

"I don't understand...."

"Oh, come on. You understand perfectly. Pawns that provide no value to the game are disposed of. They are of no use when the other game piece has won."

I gawped at him. "No..."

His expression changed suddenly, sadness and regret creeping over the hatred that previously possessed him. "I'm afraid that's how this game works, little lamb. I told you I would lead you to your slaughter... alive or dead."

"But Lola?"

He lifted his chin to look me in the eye and shook his head. "Her current bid level is far below yours. I'm afraid her end is as near as yours."

"But that's stupid. Why? I'm dead in a few weeks anyway. She may as well win the game. I'm of no use." My fingers grabbed at his shirt as I fought for Lola's life. "I'm dead anyway. Does my buyer know that?"

"He does."

"And yet he chooses to still bid? How bloody stupid is he?"

He seized the tops of my arms in both hands, his grip firm and unyielding as he shook me slightly. "Mae, calm down."

"What? How can you even...?"

His thunderous expression fixed on me as he hissed out his next words. "Some people are twisted.

They desire the possession of something... unusual. How the hell do you think snuff films are made, Mae?"

My whole world crumbled around me. I was to be purchased to create a snuff movie. "Oh my God." I suddenly struggled to breathe. "Please, Master. Oh God, no you can't let them..."

His palm fired heat across my cheek, the sting from my tears intensifying the pain. "Enough!"

The door opened once more and Master Robert stood glaring at the pair of us. "Is there some sort of problem, Daniel? Does your subject require further discipline?"

I couldn't remove my eyes from Master Daniel as I begged him to help me. He refused to acknowledge me as he kept his face on his father. "No problem, Father. We were just discussing a few regulations about behaviour tonight."

My body had shifted into shock. I couldn't move from beside my Master. Sensing my incapacity, he curled his arm around my waist to support me as he led me into the room behind his father.

Chapter Seventeen

'Help is a hindrance.'

I didn't look around the room as we entered. I couldn't focus on anything past what Master had just divulged. Horrific scenes played out in my head, movies already in the making inside my sick, twisted imagination.

Pressure built within my body, turmoil and grief overriding my system. I needed relief; I needed the serenity that only a blade could provide.

I pondered on the idea of misbehaving, knowing that would bring on Master Robert's wrath before an opportunity arose to open my veins and release some of the harrowing agony coursing through me.

I climbed up onto the podium without a second thought. I allowed Master to direct me. The only thing I could concentrate on was the fill and emptying of air into my lungs.

I heard him tut at my unladylike scale of the plastic tower but I wasn't even sure how to climb the damn thing with any elegance.

Lola shifted on her pedestal beside me. I turned to her but she remained transfixed, her gaze on nothing even though her eyes locked on something. "Lola, hi."

She didn't acknowledge me. I hissed when Master's fingers dug into my shin. "You will remain quiet throughout the dinner. You will speak only when spoken to and you will submit to any order given by any of my guests tonight. Is that understood?"

I slowly turned my eyes from Lola to him, scoffing in disgust as I looked at him with hatred. "Why not just end me now?" I rolled my eyes and huffed dramatically. "Oh sorry, I forgot. How silly of me, I'm worth a little more alive than I am dead. You can't film a slaughter if the main character is already dead."

He swallowed heavily as though my words hurt him. I winced when he exhaled and leaned into me, his fingers straightening out my dress that wasn't even creased. I realised he was making it look to the others as though he was preparing me for their liking. "I'm going to do something that I have never done before, Mae."

I frowned at him but looked down at my dress, lowering my hands to smooth out the material with him whilst he covertly spoke to me. "There is a reason I need you to behave." He paused, making sure he had my full attention. "It seems your purchaser likes your unruly behaviour. The reason for your high bid is because he apparently likes a woman with a bit of bite and fight. You are perfect material for the type of film he wants to make."

I tried to swallow the gasp that was fighting its way up my throat.

"Do you understand what I'm telling you, lamb?"

"Yes," I whispered as quietly as I could. I pulled the ribbon that doubled as a belt into a straight bow. "Yes, I understand Master."

I jolted slightly when his fingers skimmed over mine, the pad of his thumb tickling along the edge of my own. "Let's start to drop those fucking bids, little lamb. Always trust the shepherd who tries to protect you. It's not just his job, it's his..."

"Daniel?" Master Robert barked from across the room, his stern voice jerking us both from our own private moment.

I gave him a small nod of understanding before he turned back to his father.

I finally looked at my surroundings. The room was as I remembered but with a few more furnishings. Mine and Lola's podiums were positioned against the back wall on full display for the guests. The sofas had been pushed against the other walls and a large rectangular dining table sat in the centre of the large room. Place settings for six had been formally placed, each row of cutlery telling me there were five courses to be served.

Numerous people hovered around the room, talking amongst themselves. Master Daniel and Master Robert were deep in conversation with two elderly gentlemen and the Demi-whore was flirting with a man whose back was to me. I curled my lip at the way she expertly played him. The way she flicked her hair, the way she frequently touched his arm and giggled and genuinely seemed interested in him showed me just how much of an expert at seduction she was. But hey, weren't whores supposed to be good at their jobs?

"Gentlemen," Master announced. "If you would care to take a seat, dinner is ready to be served."

I roved my eyes around the room as they all shifted into position. Soft music played in the background providing a lighter atmosphere than what they were actually here for.

"It's about time!" one of the stout older men barked, causing both Lola and I to jump in surprise. "I'm rather eager to get to dessert."

My breath stilled when he looked over at me, a revolting leer curling his fat pink lips. A shiver rocked through me as I regarded him with disgust. His small grey eyes devoured me as his tongue ran along one of the flabby slugs under his moustache, wetting it and triggering a wave of nausea.

"Well, fuck," I whispered to Lola. "If he's mine I'm gonna pop myself off before he even gets the chance."

I caught the roll of Lola's lips as she tried to hide her amusement. Master tipped his head calling for my attention silently. I lifted my eyes to him. He shook his head slightly as his eyes narrowed into a fierce glare.

I narrowed my eyes back. "Can you lip read?" I mouthed wondering how the hell he had heard me. He smirked at me when I blobbed my tongue at him.

Demi caught the action and I cursed myself. She glared at me, her eyes suspicious as she flicked her gaze between Master and me.

"Charles," Master spoke when he leaned towards the obese geriatric. "Your subject is Lola, on the left. Mae, whom you have your attention on, is currently under the order of Tony."

Master gestured a hand towards who I presumed to be Tony. His short black hair was all I could see as he sat with his back to me in the large high-backed chair.

"That she is." Tony spoke without looking at me. "I'm afraid you'll need a more... substantial backer if you wish to challenge me for her, Charles."

Something crawled over me when I caught Tony's accent. It sounded familiar. I frowned and tipped my head to catch more of his dialogue but he didn't speak again. Master frowned at me, his own head slightly cocked when he observed my peculiar reaction.

Lola and I were pretty much ignored for the rest of the meal. I couldn't stop the hatred curling in my gut as I witnessed an hour of Demi touching Master. She played up to him the whole time, stroking him constantly, laughing at everything he said, attempting to feed him food from her own plate as if they were on a fucking date.

Stupid fucking nauseating bitch.

My reaction to her puzzled me as much as it angered me. If I had ever felt jealousy before I would have given this feeling a name, but as I hadn't, I couldn't recognise what it was.

After-meal drinks were delivered by a couple of staff and the party shifted to the sofas. I tried to catch a glimpse of Tony; however he chose to take a seat in a dark corner, but I felt his eyes on me the whole time. I couldn't shift the feeling that something was 'off' about him. Even during their meal, although his back had been to me, his attention had very much been *on* me. It was a strange feeling, like he was sensing me instead of looking at me.

Conversation was heavy and heated between the guests, alcohol making them louder and boisterous. Lola glanced at me when the other older man whom I had heard addressed as David started to tell the whole room very loudly how he liked to *take* his conquests. His sick and twisted preference didn't seem to shock the other individuals, only myself and Lola. He spoke of numerous torturous devices that he liked to attach his *lovers* to; clamps, chains, furniture with specific torture mechanisms attached to it. One so appalling, I nearly choked on the vomit that rushed up from my stomach.

My legs were becoming numb as the familiar throb started in my head. Dizziness accompanied the usual dull headache and at one point Lola's hand shot out to steady me when I wobbled precariously on my plastic plinth. "Are you okay?" she whispered.

"No, are you?"

She shook her head from side to side only marginally so as to not alert the others' attention. "Mae, Charles frightens me."

The fear in her voice tightened my chest. Her pretty blue eyes were dull and full of horror as she watched the guests become more and more abandoned. My heart ached for her. She was to become a slave, and whereas I had the comfort of death to steal me away from what was to come, Lola didn't and tears pricked my eyes for her.

"Honestly, Lola, I'd swap you honey, but my *date* needs it to be a little more rough."

She squinted at me, shaking her head with confusion. "Rough?"

"Mmm, seems he wants to fuck me to death... literally."

He mouth dropped open as she stared at me. "What? My God, no."

I shrugged. "Don't worry. I'm dying anyway but I'll admit, I was hoping to go out a little more... nicely."

"Oh my God, Mae. We need to get out of here."

Her wide eyes snapped around the room as if looking for an escape route. I grabbed at her hand, attempting to calm her down. She was going to get herself into deep trouble if she carried on. She was wired, running on adrenaline as terror morphed into instinct and the need to run.

"Lola, calm down, love. I'm doing what I can but you need to calm down. Master Robert is one sick crazy bastard and if he..."

"Is there a problem over there?" Demi cut in loudly.

Lola's eyes widened even further in panic when she knew what would come from our disobedience.

"Nope!" I answered, trying to bring the attention on myself. Lola wasn't coping too well and any more emotion in her blood stream wouldn't bode too well for her.

Demi narrowed her eyes on me, but her lips twisted into a cruel smirk. "I would say it's time to play gentlemen. Your subjects seem to be getting a little bored."

Charles stood up immediately, rubbing his hands together in delight as he grinned at Lola. She whimpered beside me. I loathed the sound; it stabbed at my insides.

I stared at Demi, debating whether to jump off the bloody pedestal and knock the fucking bitch out. I had never hated anyone as much in my life.

An idea formed in my head and I started to chuckle. "Demi." Her eyes widened as I spoke, shocked at my stupid bravery. "I'd love to play. You're right, I'm getting a little bored here. The only lady in the room, aside from Lola, and all you gentlemen choose to ignore me."

Master shot out of his chair. He was furious but I laughed even harder. "Bring it the fuck on!"

Shock rendered him immobile for a moment as he gawped at me. Hilarity took over as I watched him freeze. "Come on," I urged as I jumped down from the podium.

"Mae, what the hell are you doing?" Lola hissed.

I turned to look at her. "Getting the leery bastards away from you. Buckle up, baby, shit's about to hit the fan." She stared at me with as much shock as the rest of the room. "Fuck this," I goaded. "I'll start without you then."

I looked down at the front of my dress. The delicate lace neckline taunted me so I grabbed it and tore at it, ripping it into shreds until I stood before the room in half-bra and thongs, my feet still locked into my crippling red heels.

Master shook his head as his face reddened. Master Robert charged towards me but everything slammed to a halt when Tony stepped out from the darkness.

"Touch her and I will reverse every single bid I have made over the previous three years."

I didn't focus on the rest of the room when everything whooshed towards me. My legs finally gave way and I sank to the floor when my eyes landed on the man who had bought me. He shook his head in warning as he walked towards me, his eyes telling me to keep quiet and pretend.

Holy fucking shit!

Chapter Eighteen

'Guardian Angels come in many forms.'

I stared at him. I couldn't get anything to work. My heart was pounding as tears stung my eyes. "What...?"

Tony ignored me and turned to Master. "I require time alone with my subject."

Master narrowed his eyes suspiciously. "I'm afraid..."

"I am not interested in no, Daniel. I'm paying over six hundred thousand pounds for your stock, I think I am entitled to a God damned taster before you damage the goods, so to speak."

"I'm not sure Mae is experienced enough yet to submit to any sexual connection with you."

Tony laughed loudly. "And yet you still refuse my request."

"Daniel," Master Robert warned sternly.

"Fine." Master held up his hands in defeat. "If you would care to follow me, Tony. I'll provide you with a private room."

I still remained in a heap on the floor looking up at Tony in shock. "Get up!" he demanded. When I simply blinked at him he took a handful of my hair and yanked me upright. "Don't fucking defy me, girl. You won't like the consequences of your insolence."

The pain from his grip snapped me out of the daze controlling me. I winced when pain tore through the roots on my head. He dragged me after him, his large strides after Master wide and firm as he overpowered me. I tried to turn to Lola to make sure she was okay but Tony's hold restricted any movement.

We followed Master into a small room off the main hallway. He flicked on the lights then turned to Tony. "I'm afraid I can only grant you a few moments. I don't need to remind you that she isn't quite yet your possession."

Tony scoffed and quirked an eyebrow. "Well if you hurry the fuck up with the auction then she actually will be. May *I remind you* that it is only your inability to train your stock proficiently that is delaying the transaction?"

Anger contorted Master's face before he took a step towards Tony. "I can always withdraw the auction. You may be the highest bidder, Tony, but Mae is still in my guardianship until completion."

Tony straightened his back and mirrored Master's stance, taking a step towards his adversary. "I think your father may have something to say about a cancellation, Daniel. After all, this isn't your transaction to revoke but his." He tilted his head mockingly and smirked. "I would say your hands are rather tied."

Master's wrath was choking in the small room, testosterone stifling the oxygen until it became difficult to breathe. He had no choice but to relent as he turned to me. "Mae." I looked up at him from my kneeling position on the floor beside Tony, his fingers still twisted tightly in my hair. "You will behave impeccably. Do not fight or curse. Do you understand?"

I didn't miss the message in his words. "Yes, Master. I understand."

He gave me a worried glance before he turned back to Tony. "I trust you will be delivering Mae's punishment for her belligerent behaviour."

Tony smiled slyly. "Yes, very much so. I'm quite looking forward to it."

Master's face tightened as his teeth sank into his lower lip. "Then I put my faith in your self-control and trust you not to go too far. After all, you can't film a slaughter if the main character is already dead." I snapped my eyes to his when he repeated my words from earlier. He didn't acknowledge me but fixed Tony with a stare before he left the room and closed the door behind him.

I gasped when Tony hauled me upright and pushed me back against the wall. Fear and panic mixed with uncertainty and hope concocting a chaotic cocktail of emotion. I looked into his eyes but he sneered at me and brought his face closer to mine until his breath rushed over my ear.

"Play along. We are being watched. I'm sorry to do this but I have to make it look as realistic as possible Mae."

I froze when his hand covered my breast and his fingers dug into my flesh viciously. "I..."

"Sshhh. I gather you recognise me?"

"Yes." I shivered when he dipped his finger into my bra and ran the tip over my nipple. I noticed he moved slightly to the side giving our voyeurs a show. "I wasn't sure if you would, it's been nine years. We don't have much time so I'm going to be as quick as I can."

I closed my eyes and remained frozen when he slid his hand down my body until he cupped my sex over my knickers. "Once again I apologise for touching you. The deal is almost done." He ran his tongue down the length of my neck, perfecting his character. "But I'm afraid I can't get you out until the auction is completed, until money is exchanged. I am trying like hell to hurry that procedure along for you but Daniel seems to be bringing forward excuse after excuse."

He turned me around so my back was to his front. I placed my palms on the wall to steady myself as he pushed into me and pressed his mouth once more to my ear. He started to grind against me as his fingers curled around the front of my throat. "Your father was the best partner I had, Mae. We've been watching this organisation for around five years and then suddenly your face appeared on their veiled auction site. Well, you can imagine my shock."

I nodded as he took my hands and held them tight behind my back in an awkward position, the strain on my shoulders painful. "Yes, but…"

"Listen to me." I nodded, allowing him to continue. "The trade is due to take place in five days. Can you hang on until then?"

"Tony," I whispered urgently. "You need to forget me and bid for Lola. Please. They'll kill her when she loses the game. I'm dead anyway but you need to get her out of here."

"Don't worry about Lola. She'll be safe. We'll get her out as soon as the money is transferred and they accept payment."

"But it will be too late by then. As soon as you win they will kill her. Please, Tony."

"Mae, I need you to trust me. Lola will be safe and these men will be going away for a very long time."

Something shifted in my belly, a sliver of worry as Master's fate upset me. Why the hell I cared was beyond me but the thought of him going to prison left me feeling cold. "Tony, Daniel isn't a bad person. His father is..."

"What the hell, Mae? He's done nothing but humiliate and beat you. He's been involved in this venture for many years, feeding his greed with numerous auctions. You have no idea how sick and twisted he is. Don't defend him." He sighed and turned me round to face him. He kissed my cheek, little soft kisses until he worked his way back to my ear. "I believe you are suffering from Stockholm syndrome but there will be little time to give you any counselling."

He moved his lips over mine, hovering over me. "I'll make sure your last days are as comfortable as they can be. I owe you that much. You deserve that much." His eyes held mine, sadness carried in his soft expression. "I'm so sorry, Mae."

"That's okay. I'm ready to be with my parents and Connie. They are more than ready to accept me back as well."

He swallowed as he ran his thumb over my cheekbone. "You are one strong woman. Your parents would be proud of you."

I answered him with a small smile.

The door reopened and Tony shifted back from me. He turned towards Master with a smug grin. "She tastes exquisite and will be perfect for what we need. I'll make the necessary arrangements for five days' time. We don't have much time to record before she dies so I'm relying on you to complete this damn transaction without any more hitches."

Master simply nodded, regarding Tony with slightly narrow eyes. "Five days will be sufficient time to finish her course."

"Good, because I won't wait much longer. If she dies in the meantime then I'll have to transfer the bids over to the other girl, but that would be a shame. Mae is simply perfect. Her looks and specifically her scar will drive our clientele wild. She already has that victim appearance, and vulnerability sells."

I gawped at him, only just holding myself back from hitting him when I realised he was playing a part. The way Master growled at him caused both Tony and me to stare in shock. Tony stepped backwards when Master stepped angrily towards him. "I suggest you leave before I annul this fucking deal, with or without my father's consent."

"Master?'

He blinked and looked at me then seemed to realise what he was doing and shook himself. "It is time for Mae to retire for the night. I'll show you out,

Tony." He turned to me. "I'll see you in your room shortly, Mae."

I nodded. "Of course, Master." I hurried from the room commanding myself not to glance Tony's way and ruin his cover.

Excitement bubbled in my belly. I just hoped that Tony managed to get me out before it all went to hell. At least I was guaranteed to die by cancer instead of killed off in some freak bloody movie. I was concerned for Lola though. I had a bad feeling that as soon as the transaction took place that they would end her life. Although Tony had promised me he would help her, I wasn't sure he would manage to save her in time.

I was ready for him when he entered my room. I secured my gaze on a portion of the wall as I knelt in preparation. I sensed his fury as he slowly walked towards me. His thighs blocked my line of sight and I forced myself not to drool over the way his trousers sheathed the thick muscles, the outline showing me how perfect his legs were.

"Who is he?"

My heart thundered wildly. I was sure he could smell the perspiration that broke out in droplets over my forehead. "My buyer."

I flinched when he dropped to his haunches in front of me. He was silent and I kept my eyes on his chest. "Don't lie to me, lamb."

"I'm not, Master. You have been dealing with him, he's purchasing me." I lifted my eyes to his. "So he can torture me to death."

His jaw hardened as anger blazed in his eyes. I cried out when his hand circled my throat and he lifted me up, forcing me onto the bed. My back slapped the duvet, my body bouncing back up with the force of his throw.

He was above me before I could blink, his huge body taking mine prisoner underneath him. "Don't fucking lie to me!"

"I'm not!" I shouted back, my throat straining under the tightness of his hold.

"Is he a lover?"

"What the hell? No!"

"There's something you're not telling me, Mae. And believe me, if I find out for myself what is going on then you'll regret ever fucking meeting me."

I scoffed. "I already fucking regret ever meeting you!"

I braced for his hand to connect with my cheek but it didn't. The only sound was both of our heavy breaths as we stared each other out and strived to control the hatred suffocating our emotions.

I froze when his hand slid up the middle of my breastbone and circled my throat. "Tell me how you know him, lamb." His tone was softer this time, the tightness in his throat echoing an emotion that, if I didn't know him, would have sounded much like hurt.

"I don't know him."

"He was very intimate with you."

I couldn't grasp what he was insinuating. Why he seemed to be more concerned if I'd had a relationship with him instead of anything else he could have posed a concern for. "I don't understand what you want from me."

His hand slid higher up my neck until he cupped my chin, his hold gentle as his long fingers framed my jawline. "Tell me, Mae." His eyes secured mine, the rich chocolate swirling expressively as he gazed at me. "How many men have you had?"

My eyes widened. "What?"

His thumb stroked along my bottom lip, removing all the moisture. He dropped his eyes to watch my tongue recoat my lips. "How many lovers have you had?"

My mouth dried when he didn't remove his gaze from it; he seemed enthralled by my lips. "I..."

"You?" he encouraged when his eyes lifted back to mine.

"I'm not sure what concern it is of yours how many *lovers* I've had?"

"I'm not talking about boyfriends, Mae. I know there have been none. I mean one night stands, lovers, pleasure seekers. Just tell me."

I huffed and scowled at him. "Fine. I haven't had any lovers."

He tilted his head questioningly. "Now we both know that's a lie. For one, there is me."

I spat out a bitter laugh. "I wouldn't call you a lover, Master. Far from it."

His gaze darkened but he remained above me, my body still pinned under his and my face still captured in his hold. "And you see, that's where I'm having trouble. So you've only ever had sex with me, lovers or not."

"Yes," I snapped. "And we mustn't forget your father now."

His eye twitched as a slight tic contorted the muscle in his cheek. "Yes, and my father," he growled out. "That is what troubles me."

"I don't follow."

He cocked his head almost sinisterly, his eyes burning with something I hadn't witnessed before. "You're very inexperienced, and yet your purchaser touches you and you barely even flinch. I'd have expected you of all people to put up a bit of a fight. You gave my father one and you certainly gave me one. Yet Tony, a man who threatens to kill you and film it, a man who pays thousands of pounds for the pleasure of fucking you to an extreme level should have disgusted you more than ever."

I stared at him. I was sure he could feel the thunder that was cracking behind my breasts as my chest heaved beneath him. "Well," I spoke as calmly as possible. "I've realised that there's no point in fighting anymore. It doesn't get me anywhere, only more pain."

He smirked. "So if I was to take you right here, right now, you wouldn't so much as bat an eyelid?"

I wasn't sure what was happening. Repulsion surged through me but it was slowly pushed aside by another sensation that filled me when Master pushed his erection into my lower stomach. "If I stripped you naked and ran my touch all over your exquisite soft skin then you wouldn't do a thing to stop me?"

"No," I whispered. A shudder ripped through me when he lowered his face towards mine. His breath smelt of the red wine he'd drunk earlier, a hint of sweet potato tickling my nostrils with how close he was.

"And if I ran my tongue all the way from here..." The tip of his tongue tickled the skin just under my ear. I swallowed back the moisture that filled my mouth when he very slowly trailed it along my jawline and down the centre of my throat. "...To here." He lifted his eyes to me. "You wouldn't fight me?"

I quirked a brow. "Did I just fight you?"

"No," he breathed as he brought his mouth to my face, his lips directly hovering over mine. "No, you didn't. But that tells me nothing. That just tells me you're aroused by me, that you wouldn't protest in the slightest should I turn you over beneath me and fuck you hard and fast."

I tried to control the gasp that wanted to escape. I swallowed it back but that just changed it into a tight whimper. He chuckled as he slid his hand down the middle of my chest again. "I wonder if your nipples are hard, Mae."

I closed my eyes as he slid his palm over my right breast, his touch incredibly hot. My nipples seemed to reach for him, peaking under the soft material of my nightdress. He locked me down in his stare as he slowly traced around my hard bud with the tip of his finger. My body was going wild, each nerve ending screaming for more, each tiny hair on my body raised in expectation as moisture saturated my thighs.

I huffed when he pinched my nipple roughly, his thumb and finger pinching and rolling as my hips involuntary rose towards him in search of some sort of stimulant.

"I..." I lost control of my words, they shot up my throat then decided, fuck it, and hurried back down. My mind swayed when he ran his tongue across my bottom lip and tickled my nipple, barely touching but sending shots of fire down to my pussy.

"What do you want, Mae?" he whispered over my mouth.

I whimpered, refusing the forbidden words to surface, but they, like everything else in my life, refused my appeal. "I want you to kiss me."

His eyes snapped wider, his stare now stern and heated. He shook his head and laughed cruelly. "Ahh, lamb, over everything I can do for you... *to you*, you want me to kiss you?" His words mocked me and I blinked back the hurt.

"No, I..." I refused the tears that wanted to pool, forcing them back as I stared at him. "No." I couldn't seem to find the words to fire back at him, to hurt him with so I just turned my face away from his. "Just rape me and have it over with."

He reared back, incredulity slapped on his face. "What the...?" He scrambled from the bed, anger now drowning the softness that had been in his eyes. "Why are you always so bloody unpredictable?"

Whoa!

Anger flooded me and I shot off the bed. My mouth opened and closed as his bewilderment floored me. "Do you...? Jesus bloody Christ, you are unreal!" I ignored the shadow that crossed his face, I was too damn angry. "I'm unpredictable? *I'm* unpredictable? What the hell do you expect from me? Eh? You showed me something good inside you three years ago, made me trust you, even like you, and you turned out to be the very thing my father had taught me to watch out for. But yeah, as usual, stupid Mae had been blind, unfocussed on what you really were because *I actually liked you*." I stormed towards him when he remained still, his fists by his side, his jaw as hard as his stare. "You didn't just take my virginity that night. You took my life, my soul. You ripped out my heart, tore it to pieces right in front of me. You left me more than just broken, you left me dead inside. But then... then you gave me so much more and still, even after you gave, you took."

Blasts of his breath swarmed my face as he furiously strove to control his breathing. "And then when you decided to step up your sick fucking game, you came back. Just when I had the chance to finally leave this shit fucking God dammed planet, you took my final moments here and crucified them." I pushed at his chest, causing him to stumble back slightly.

I was too far gone to stop, my mind racing as words scurried out in anger. He was right in front of me, virtually nose to nose as I leaned into his face. "You raped my body, you raped my spirit, you raped my life and now... now you even rape my death!"

"Have you finished?" He spoke through his teeth, his voice tight.

I shook my head sadly. "What's the fucking point? There is none. Whatever happens, I'm dead. I would have just liked my final moments to be spent with someone who actually liked me, maybe even... even..."

"Even?" he asked quietly when my sobs choked the words.

"It doesn't matter."

I turned my back to him, walking over to the door. He didn't stop me from opening it or walking through it. He didn't stop me as he followed me along the hallway, nor did he stop me when I walked into the correction centre.

He stood, regarding me silently when I walked over to the wooden cross on the wall. I ripped off my nightgown, tossing it on the floor beside me before I bent and shackled my ankles into the straps at the base of the cross. I fixed one wrist into the right cuff. "You'll have to secure my other wrist." My voice seemed strange, almost ghostly.

He didn't move but I could sense him behind me, watching my strange behaviour. My body was humming in so much pain that I needed more pain to release it. I needed the splitting of skin and the spilling of blood to bate the intolerable pressure building through my system. Blood scorched my veins as it bubbled like a volatile volcano threatening release. "Please... just fucking finish me."

I could hear him breathing, the rapid intake and exit of air through his nose as his rage tickled my sensitive skin. "Come on, Daniel. You wanna hurt me, then fucking hurt me."

I closed my eyes when he suddenly appeared and snapped my other wrist angrily into the buckle. Time seemed to still as slave manipulated her Master, twisted his emotions until he gave her exactly what she wanted.

I heard him unhook one of the whips from the wall but still he was silent. My body braced when he shifted behind me. "Hurt me, damn it," I begged when nothing happened, when all he did was stand behind me and observe.

The pain was growing unbearable and I needed to do something quick before my skin ripped open by itself to release the vacuum of energy crippling me. "FUCKING DO IT!" I screamed. I smiled when words formed in my head. "Punish me for wanting to fuck my buyer like I never had before. Hurt me for wanting to take my buyer's cock in my mouth and swallow his cum just like I did yours. Make me pay for wanting to ride him hard and brutally." But then my treacherous words betrayed me. "Make me bleed for how much I want you to take me, how desperate I am to take your cock inside me. How much I need you to fuck me..."

That did it.

The first crack released so many blissful endorphins into my brain that my eyes rolled and my body sagged in relief. The second and third strike empowered the ecstasy until all that ruled me was pleasure and calm. The fourth and fifth made my body pulse with heat as the pain transformed into arousal.

Each time the slash of leather stole my skin, a rush of release like never before flowed through me. My belly throbbed, my pussy pulsed, my nipples swelled. My brain fought to cope with the pain until it no longer recognised it and masked it as something completely different.

I hadn't noticed the thrashing had finished until I felt Master push up against me. My eyes widened when he thrust inside me, his large cock stretching me wide and burning my internal walls with delicious pain. "You want fucking, Mae? Eh? Is this what you want?"

His thrusting was animalistic and frenzied, his balls slapping against the tops of my thighs as he rammed into me. A shiver of heaven shook my body when he took a large clump of hair and pulled so hard I thought my neck would snap. "Tell me, Mae!"

The cuffs tore at the skin on my wrists as my Master refused me any time to register the moment. His banged me harder and harder against the cross until I finally shifted my face to the side so he didn't break my nose. "Yes!"

"You want more?"

"Fuck yes! Give me more, please."

He didn't refuse me, he gave me exactly what I wanted, what I needed. "He can never give you this, lamb. He can never give you what you crave."

His words hardly registered as I took the pleasure he gave me. I jerked my hips back against him, the exquisite rush of pleasure electrifying me as the action pulled his thick cock deeper inside me.

Pressure starting building again, but this time it was a hot pressure, an intense throb of sensation. "Oh, God!"

I was instantly snapped out of the restraints and forced to the floor. "Sula!" he barked as he towered over me.

I turned onto my back immediately, opening my legs to him as I spread my arms out beside me.

He dropped to his knees between my thighs. My eyes locked onto his as he shifted over the top of me. My chest stuttered when he forced himself back inside me. "You're so fucking tight, little lamb."

I nodded but didn't reply as my back arched in instant delight to the fill of him once again. He watched me, his eyes on my face as he knelt between my legs and fucked me hard. The position he was in made the head of his cock scrape over a part inside me that shot a ripple of pleasure through me every time he stroked it.

My eyes closed as my body prepared itself to let go. "Look at me, Mae. Look who is inside you. Look at who owns you."

"You don't own me," I growled out defiantly. My words belied the need. He did very much own me in that moment. I would allow him anything if he made this intense buzz inside me shift into the surge of bliss I knew could take over.

But he slowed down, almost stopped. His thrusts were still hard and deep but the friction was gone. Each slow pass of his cock over my sweet spot drove me crazy. "I'll always own you, Mae Swift." The way he looked at me caused an eruption of emotion in my chest. "You know why?"

I shook my head. A tear rolled from the edge of my eye when he stroked his palm softly over my cheek. "Because I'll be the last person who is ever inside you."

"But..."

He thrust hard, causing me to yelp and groan in pleasure. "Have you ever been loved, lamb?"

Pain reared its ugly head. "Yes."

He narrowed his eyes. "Not your parents or sister. Have you ever been in love?"

I shook my head once again. "No."

His movements inside me deepened but each slow slide of his cock brought on a new ecstasy when he almost removed himself then slipped back in just as slowly. I struggled for breath as something shifted between us. He brought his face lower. "I'm going to kiss you like you've never been kissed before."

And he did exactly that. The soft way in which he controlled me burnt a hole through my soul. My mind told me it was all manipulation, but my heart knew better. It wasn't just a kiss, it was a joining, a deep connection that snaked through both of us. I felt it seep into him as it poured into me. His hands framed my face and he tilted his mouth until we were just one, both of us linked..

"Mae," he whispered on my cheek when he stiffened and swelled inside me. Warmth flooded my womb and I shivered, my own climax taking me as high as him.

A sob erupted from me. It was forbidden but very much a necessity. It broke the finality of my life. It took my soul and finally prepared it for what was to come. It had at long last seen gentleness, softness, an act of pleasure that was given not taken, and now every single part of me was ready to leave.

Chapter Nineteen

'The deliverance of truth is a risk we take.'

"Master," I whispered into the dark room. I knew he was with me, beside me. He'd picked me up from the floor after what I could only describe as 'our joining' and took me into his own bed. To say I had been shocked didn't exactly cover the emotion that had confused me.

He hadn't spoken another word and when I'd tried to say something, he'd just shaken his head, placed a finger to my lips and turned me over. His firm, warm body had slotted into the curve of my back precisely, almost as though we had been created to be placed side by side in the world. And that was all until I had woken moments ago.

"Master," I repeated almost desperately.

"What, Mae?" His tone was soft as he shifted behind me. Light blinded me and I whimpered. He shut off the lamp quickly. "Are you having an attack?"

"Mmm," I slurred. "It hurts."

"Wait a moment."

I squeezed my eyes closed in preparation for the light to flood, but it never came. Loud grunts filled the silence as Master stumbled around in the darkness. Faint bangs and curses echoed and if it wouldn't have hurt my head to laugh, I'd have been in hysterics at his blind stumbling.

"I'm slipping the door open, the light from the hallway will filter in but I'll be as quick as I can."

His consideration chipped at something hard inside me, the splinter falling into my lungs and making it difficult to breathe. I couldn't work out his sudden change. It was as if he'd had a transplant. I knew he still didn't believe me about Tony and if I was honest, I wasn't sure myself what to make of it. It wasn't a matter of hoping he would get me out in time, worry and anguish built inside me over many things. Lola was a deep fear. I needed to get her out before it all kicked off and yet I knew, deep down that she wouldn't make it.

Tears trickled across my cheeks as I once more saw her eyes, the piercing blue strength that had carried me through the horrific attack Master's father had rained over me. The way she had journeyed the terror with me, supporting me through every step had me owing her my sanity, although I wasn't quite sure how much of it I had left.

A sliver of light broke across one dark wall and I cringed when it fired shots of pain behind my eyes. Master continued to struggle in the dark until I felt something soft slide over my head. Fingers gently manoeuvred a piece of material until a shock of velvet covered my eyes. "It's just a blindfold," he whispered beside me. "Just while I put on the light to give you your medication."

I didn't answer him, it was too painful. My brain blazed, scorching agony scurrying across my scalp. I felt a slight scratch on my upper arm and then almost immediately sweet, sweet nectar as every edge of pain blurred into heavenly oblivion.

Natural light woke me, the soft rays of the morning sun creeping into the room through the slotted blinds. My head had eased, allowing me to open my eyes and take stock of the room I was in.

Muted colours painted the walls with matching subdued grey furnishings. The furniture was sparse, cold and clinical in blacks and even more greys. No decoration or ornament broke the gloom of the room as I eyed it sceptically. From what I could see, three doors were the only things that interrupted the harshness of the room.

"Hey," Master whispered softly behind me. "Better?"

"Yes." I turned over until I was facing him. "Thank you."

He smiled gently. My God, he was so utterly perfect; breath-taking. His usual angry expression was gone. Instead, a stunning softness veiled his face, making him almost angelic. His hair was severely messed, the black strands wayward and wild as his usual puckered brow appeared soft and smooth. His deep eyes pooled the rich mahogany into a lush, coffee gaze. His straight nose complimented his thick lips, the soft pink flesh turning upwards charmingly in his *real* smile.

I reached out and stroked a finger along his chin, the slight stubble tickling the pad of my finger. His gaze darkened as I touched him, his eyes blackening as his lips parted. "You should smile more often. You're so very handsome."

He frowned, showing me the customary creased forehead and the pain that lived on every single feature of his face. "The devil wears many masks, Mae."

I smiled at him. "And an angel has many personalities."

He lifted his fingers to mine, framing my hold on his face. He took my hand under him and slid it upwards into his hair. "Can you feel the horns, lamb?"

I laughed softly when he smiled again. "There's only one horn I can feel right now, and it's definitely not on your head."

His eyes widened before he laughed loudly. "And that," he grinned as he tapped my nose, "was the last thing I expected from you." He ground his erection into my lower belly with a wicked glint in his eye.

"I'm simply stating facts, Master."

He smirked and a shiver trickled down my spine as desire hung heavy between us. "And if I was to say you are wet for me, would that be stating another fact?"

"Yes."

"And if I were to lift you up and bury my face between your legs, drive my tongue hard inside you, I would taste your sweet arousal, would that be stating another fact?"

My mouth dried and I struggled to sound words. "Yes."

"And if I were to slide my finger inside your pussy and stroke that delicious little place inside you, I would make you scream for more. Would that be stating a fact?"

"Oh God, yes. Very much so."

He pushed me over until I was on my back and covered me with himself. His mouth was on mine in seconds, his tongue darting between my lips to find mine. He groaned when I fought with him, devouring his mouth as I pulled him closer by his hair. He battled back, his teeth biting as his tongue fucked my mouth. I lifted my legs, wrapping him between them so I could hold him further against me. His cock slid deliciously between my thighs, rubbing over my swollen clit and firing a blast of pleasure through me. I moaned into his mouth, asking, begging for more.

He pulled back, his eyes hard on mine. "Why?" He looked shocked at his own question and I frowned.

"Why? Why what?"

"I don't... It's just..." He gritted his teeth when the words wouldn't voice. He changed route instantly and dropped his face to my breasts. My back arched when he sucked at my nipple, drawing it deep into his warm mouth and tracing the edge with the tip of his tongue. My fingers dug into his hair, holding him in place so he would give me more.

He moved across my chest, placing gentle tiny kisses along the route until he found my other breast. My body was on fire, the need inside me increasing until it became unbearable.

"I need you." It was said with instinct, lust controlling everything in my system. It took over; craving, searching for its high, hunting for anything that could give it satisfaction, and urgency demanding the drug that pleasured. "God, I need you so much."

His heavy aroused breaths brushed down my belly as he made his way past my navel, his tongue flicking out to torment on his adventure. He practically yanked my legs apart. His gaze dropped from my face until he was staring at the most intimate part of me. I lowered my hands to cover myself, regretting it immediately when his eyes narrowed and he growled. "Never hide yourself from me, Mae. That is something I will not tolerate."

I nodded quickly, moving my hands until they dropped by my side and I fisted the bed sheet. "Oh!" I cried out when he grabbed my legs and flung them over his shoulders, the action lifting my hips off the bed and placing my pussy directly in front of his face.

"Have you ever had a man's mouth on you, lamb? His tongue in your tight little cunt?"

I looked down at him and shook my head. The smile that covered his face could only be described as completely and utterly filthy.

A shudder of pleasure rolled over me when he trailed his tongue all the way up me. "Oh, shit!" I muttered when he circled around my clit then suddenly dipped the length of his tongue inside me.

"Watch!" he demanded as he locked eyes with me.

I nodded, watching him furiously eat me. He wasn't delicate; he completely destroyed me, his mouth idolising, torturing, pleasuring, consuming until nothing existed in my head, only a deep-seated fury to climax.

I grabbed at his head, forcing him to pleasure me, demanding that he bring me off when I couldn't take any more.

"That's it, Mae. Give me what you have." He growled as my orgasm ripped into me. Every single muscle cried out in both delight and torture as my body shifted away from itself. My shoulders and my Master's shoulders were the only things supporting me as ecstasy made me fly.

He climbed up my body, placing random little kisses on his journey up. "And now it's my turn." He grinned and watched my face when he nudged his cock inside me slowly. I daren't remove my eyes from his as I watched something slide across his face. His teeth sank into his lower lip, pulling the plump flesh further into his mouth the deeper inside me he slid. "I don't know what the hell it is about you, Mae."

I lifted my hips to meet his. His deep groan matched my own as pleasure curled through us both. He started to move inside me, rocking rhythmically but gently. Each time he pushed in, I pushed towards him, loving the way his eyes glinted in pleasure as we fucked each other. Tension built in both of us as the pace increased and we drove one another hard.

He slid his hands under me, holding me to him as he rolled over. I placed my hands on his chest, my thighs clamping his waist as I stared at him. "I... I don't know what to do. I've never...."

He slid his palms up my thighs until he was holding my hips. "Take me whichever way you want, lamb. Instinct will take over."

Nerves got the better of me and I sat on him, immobilised. He smiled softly, waiting until I was ready. His cock had buried even deeper with the position and I shivered when he throbbed inside me. Lust took control and told my body what to do when I lifted gently off him. He nodded and groaned when I slowly lowered back down on him. "That's it, you got this."

I began to move faster and harder, taking from him what my body demanded until I was riding him hard. "Come here," he ordered as he gripped my arms and pulled me towards him.

My chest squashed against the deep contours of him, my nipples rubbing over his short chest hair. He pulled at my backside, opening me wider to him as he held me still and thrust frantically inside me. I growled loudly when he slipped a finger into my anus. I had never felt such extreme bliss, such a thrilling gratification as I rocked back against him. "That's it, my darling, take and give."

He started to finger my arse in rhythm to his cock fucking my pussy. The overwhelming fullness sent pulses of pleasure around my body and into my brain, taking my inhibitions and destroying them along with any pain inside my soul.

Something bubbled inside me, something deep that wanted to free itself. Unidentified words formed in my mind, pushing at my boundaries of denial as they tackled the part of me that rejected them. I couldn't allow them. They weren't the truth; I refused to let them be the truth as I searched Master's eyes. He didn't feel it, he would never feel it. I would be leaving this world unloved and alone.

He shushed me when tears slid down my face. My mind wept as heartache mixed with pleasure and an orgasm rolled over me, ravishing my body in ecstasy as my soul sobbed in sorrow. Despair blended with rapture when he yanked me harder onto him and filled me with himself. "Fuck!" he cried out as his climax unexpectedly hit. "Fuck... Mae."

I pushed onto him, draining every drop from him as a sob of sorrow brought back memories. His sperm mocked me as it reminded me.

"I..." I shook my head angrily and climbed off him. "Mae?"

I was so confused as my orgasm still held my body in a shiver of pleasure, but my mind reminded of my hatred towards the only man who had ever given me pleasure. I couldn't control the fight of emotion inside me. He hurt me but he thrilled me, he lit my body up as the disease darkened it and he fed my heart as cancer destroyed my brain.

"There's something I need to tell you," I whispered, refusing to turn around. I didn't want to see his face when I told him.

"Mae?"

I heard him shuffle behind me. I stiffened when he gently took my shoulders and tried to turn me around.

"No, I can't..."

"What is it? Tell me."

"I...God damn..." My heart was screaming at me to tell him as my mind told me to shut the fuck up. I didn't know what would become of my truths. Would it cause deeper despair or could I leave knowing that I had done the right thing?

"Are you scared?"

I turned to him. "Of death?"

"Yes."

"Not especially. I'm terrified of dying in pain but as for the actual thing, then no. I'm ready for whatever comes after... this."

His expression saddened, and I softly cupped his face. He nuzzled into me and kissed the palm of my hand. "I've never..." I waited for him to continue but he shook his head and smiled. "If you had the choice and could decide your own fate and leave when you want to, would you?"

I nodded. "Yes. That's what frightens me, having no control over it. I want to go on my terms. I'm ready and waiting, and while God prefers to play with my life, the lingering is crippling me."

He placed his hand over mine. "Your strength astounds me. Your acceptance and understanding aches at me. I know why you never fought, lamb, why you accepted your fate and prepared for it, and I wish beyond anything that there was something in this life that could have made you fight and hold on."

"There was only ever one thing that battled with that decision."

He frowned, his head cocked slightly. "And that is?"

I paused as I swallowed back the worry, but I needed to free the truth and have faith for the first time in my life, and hope I was doing the right thing.

A tear raced down my face as images flashed behind my eyes and my heart cried out. "We have a daughter."

Chapter Twenty

'In to Hell Heaven drags us.'

He stared at me. His face was unemotional, and if it wasn't for the slight tic in his right cheek I would have thought he hadn't heard me. My heart raced uncontrollably in my chest, blood rushing through my system, making me lightheaded.

"You're lying," he hissed as he snapped his fingers around my upper arms. "You are lying." He shook me so hard my brain bounced around my skull, knocking the swollen part until agony pierced my pain barrier. I squinted at him as nausea threatened. "WHY?"

"I'm not lying to you."

"You must be. I have watched you, every year, I watched you. I have never witnessed a child."

"She was born November the fifth, bonfire night. Six weeks before your first annual visit."

I watched as different questions crossed his face, each as confusing as the last. The first was as I had expected. "Where is she?"

"It doesn't matter where she is. You will never see her."

Fury erupted from him and he was instantly upon me, my back slamming the wall as he imprisoned me under him. His fingers circled my throat tightly but I took his rage, devoured it, because it was the only thing that overruled the pain in my heart.

"Where – is – she?"

His grip tightened until all I could do was allow it. His eyes blazed as furious torrents of hot air raged from his nostrils. He screamed and dropped me. He paced across the room as he ran his fingers through his thick hair, turning it into a nest of chaotic black disarray. He turned to me with narrow eyes. "Are you sure she's mine?"

My jaw dropped. "How dare you! You really think that after what you did to me that I would go out and seek lovers?"

"I obviously know nothing about you, Mae."

I scoffed and shook my head. "I am a woman, Master. I'm sorry for the way my body works, but did you never consider the outcome of raping someone without using protection? I mean, it wasn't as though I had a choice in the matter, but you did."

He ran his hands over his face and groaned. "Sweet fucking Jesus. I..."

"You what? You actually care about another human being, child or adult? No, you don't so don't even pretend to care where she is."

He spun round. "You know nothing about me, Mae. You have no idea what I feel or don't feel."

"So come on then, surprise me. Who do you care about, other than yourself, that is?"

"I..." His mouth snapped closed as soon as it had opened. He blinked furiously then inhaled and sank onto the bottom of the bed. "How am I supposed to care for my child when I knew nothing of her existence? Tell me that."

I couldn't answer his question but I had one of my own. "Are you even capable of caring? Of loving?"

His eyes shot up to mine. He paused, reaching inside me with his gaze. "Yes, Mae. I am very much capable of loving."

His words brought a shiver and I turned from him, not allowing him to see the thoughts in my head. "Well she's cared for. Something I am unable to do."

"Did you know of your tumour when you had her?"

"No." I shook my head and sighed. "But I couldn't give her much and she deserved to have more than the horror that brought her into this world. She must never know how she was created. That is something I won't spoil her with."

He nodded. "Do you see her?"

I swallowed back the bile of sorrow. "No. She is too innocent to see me. I am a phantom of her nightmares and she deserves dreams and fairy-tales."

"You gave her away?"

"No, I didn't," I snapped. "I gave her a chance at life. I killed myself to give her a life with someone who can give her the good things in life. I destroyed myself when I handed her over so don't you dare fucking judge me."

He shook his head briskly. "I'm not judging you, Mae."

He lifted from the bed and walked towards me. I swiped at the tears that fell. He stood before me and turned my face back to his when I refused to look at him. His hand pressed against the side of my face as his thumb wiped away the wetness from my cheeks. "What have I done to you?" he whispered.

My heart cracked and I gazed at him. "You decimated me, Daniel. You annihilated every single good part of me and structured hatred. I'm glad I'm dying because there is only so much abhorrence you can live with until you become an abomination of existence."

"You never stood a chance, Mae. He wanted you with a debilitating need."

"Who did?" I questioned. "I don't understand."

He shook his head and turned again. I watched as he opened one of the doors and disappeared inside. Everything was numb, blurred around the edges. His confusing declaration didn't make any sense.

"Who wanted me?" I asked again as I stood at the door to his walk-in wardrobe and watched him pull on numerous clothes.

"It doesn't matter."

"Of course it bloody matters. This is my life. If it wasn't you, then who?" He didn't answer me so I took a guess. "Your father?"

He shook his head as he pulled on a dark blue t-shirt with some foreign words emblazed on the front. I frowned deeper. I had really thought it was his father that had given the order for me to be the next auction. "You mean you work for someone else?"

Panic set in. Was Tony aware of this? He hadn't mentioned anything and now I was even more troubled. "Daniel, tell me please."

"It doesn't matter. It's done. Nothing we can do to change it now."

"No, Daniel." I didn't care that I used his name. I didn't think it even bothered him. "I need to know. It's important."

This was bigger than I thought if outsiders ran the business. I didn't even know how to alert Tony to this information but I knew within my bones that I needed to. "If it isn't your father, then who?"

He frowned, suspicious over my frantic questioning. "Why does it matter?" Suddenly his eyes widened and he grabbed at me. "Who knew about our daughter?"

I shook my head as he raged at me. What the hell? The terror on his face added to my own anguish. "Why?"

"WHO KNOWS?"

I blinked at him as he shouted at me. "I…"

"Fuck, Mae!" He was frantic, fear shaking him as he demanded an answer. I knew deep down that it was important.

"Just Spud."

He blanched, the colour on his face draining rapidly as his breathing became uncontrollable. "No!" He shook his head.

My legs wobbled and I stared wide-eyed. "No, not Spud. He's my friend!"

Anguish and guilt covered his face. "No, he isn't."

"Yes he is," I whispered as my heart broke. "He's the… only friend I have. Please don't take that from me as well."

"I'm so sorry, lamb," he whispered as he pulled me to him and placed a lingering kiss on my forehead. "He's… Spud's real name is Franco Genole. He… he…" He blew out a breath and shivered. "He… oh my God, this is so hard."

"What is? Tell me."

He took my hand and led me over to a small couch in the corner of his room. He sat me down and settled beside me, refusing to let go of my hands, his grip firm and almost painful. He swallowed again before he blew the truths of my past into smithereens.

"This... business has been operating for roughly twelve years. Franco took it over from his father. Besides what you may think, it is very, very lucrative. It earns Franco and my father millions every year." I nodded, urging him to go on. "Franco and another were the main leaders, with my father just an apprentice back then. Franco became greedy, his thirst for power and money unquenchable. "

"And you?"

He shrugged. "I was... I'm not going to lie to you, Mae. I enjoy it. I was brought in six years ago as an auctioneer and hunter."

"You hunted for victims?"

He nodded and dropped his eyes. "Yes. I hunt for girls that I know will make us a lot of money at auction. I prowl parties, universities, bars, even local parks."

I nodded as nausea curled deep. "But why rape them?"

"Because it destroys them."

"What the..."

"It's part of the game, Mae. The destruction. I rape them, plant the device that allows me to grant access to them. Their lives are recorded immediately, their stats and images uploaded onto the website so buyers bid immediately. The bids grow in retrospect to how the stocks... sorry victims, to how they deal with life after. If they sink, they don't make it far but the ones like you, who fight back, they entice the buyers, turn them on. I believe that is why you saw an overwhelming amount of bids."

I stared at him. I couldn't find words to voice how I was feeling. "Why... me? Why did you choose me?"

"That's just it." He shook his head. "I didn't. For the first time ever I was sent to you specifically. I'd watched you for a while, wondering what it was about you that Franco wanted. Yes, you're beautiful and strong but I'd never been given an actual target before."

"It doesn't make sense."

He sighed and lifted my hands to his mouth. He kissed my knuckles and swallowed. "Franco's partner in the early years was..." He closed his eyes. "Your father."

I screamed at him and slapped his face, pulling my hands out of his. "Don't fucking lie. It's you! It's you who's done this. You..." I punched at him, desperately trying to hurt him as his lies finally murdered my soul, burned it within me until all that was left was dust and agony. "Don't lie to make yourself look better. He was a cop, a damn good one."

He grabbed at my wrists, his fingers holding me in a vice as he attempted to control me. "I'm not lying. Your father came across Franco's operation in the early days. But instead of reporting it, ending it, he fed the damn thing and made it what it is. He was the brains behind it."

"NO!"

"Yes, Mae. I'm sorry. I'm so sorry but now we have to face the fact we have a bigger problem."

"No." I grabbed at him frantically. "Oh God, no. Don't let him hurt her, Daniel. Please. I don't understand what he has against me if my father worked with him."

He looked away. "Your father fell in love with a particular girl."

I blinked. "What? He loved my mother."

Daniel shrugged. "That is irrelevant. He fell in love with Franco's wife."

My eyes closed slowly as understanding slid in. "All this for revenge?"

"I'm afraid so. Your parents didn't die in a one off car crash, lamb."

It was all becoming too much. My head throbbed as my brain struggled with knowledge and hidden truths. "I..." I sagged as numbness overwhelmed me. "My whole life, since my parents' death, all I've had was the memories. The happy moments in my childhood that filled the emptiness inside me. And now, now I won't even get to leave with those."

He was silent for a moment but then he looked at me. "Then we create some more before it's too late."

"What?"

He jumped up off the bed almost excitedly. "Pack a bag with everything you can."

"Eh?" I stared at him in confusion.

He didn't answer straight away as he disappeared into his wardrobe. "I said, pack a bag. We're leaving."

"Can we... do that?"

"No," he answered immediately. "But we are."

Chapter Twenty One

'Hiding reveals what we bury deep.'

Daniel had brought us to an insanely beautiful cabin deep in the woods somewhere rural and quiet. After bundling me into his car, we hadn't stopped until he pulled up a dirt track and we arrived at the cabin several hours later. I had begged him to go back for Lola but he'd shaken his head and told me he'd sorted it. I wasn't sure how he had sorted it but he'd disappeared for an hour before he'd fetched me from my room and led me from a house I never wanted to see again.

"Wow. It's beautiful."

He smiled and nodded, sighing deeply as though the place calmed him. "Yes. It was my mother's."

I returned his smile with the gentle way he referred to his mother. "Is she... dead?"

He nodded once and I knew that was all I was to hear about her. Sadness weighed heavy as I watched his soft smile disappear and pain replace it. It was obviously a hard subject and I didn't press; he was entitled to his own memories.

He took my hand and pulled me up the small gravel path. He pulled out a key, unlocking the door and took us both through into a small square foyer.

Daniel instantly started to pull dust sheets from the furniture and after I helped him we unveiled the house within an hour. I had discovered a stunning house, with rich and comfortable furnishings that didn't reek of expense and wealth. Cosiness and contentment governed instead of showiness and fickle status.

"Eat," Daniel ordered as he held another olive to my lips.

"I can't." I laughed as I placed a hand on my stuffed belly and leaned back in the chair. "Are you trying to fatten me up before my slaughter?"

It was meant as a joke but the way his face darkened with anger halted my laughter. "I'm sorry." He nodded as he popped a piece of cheese in his mouth and studied me. "Can I ask you something?"

"Of course." He grinned. "Although I can't promise to answer."

I shifted in my chair so I was facing him and drew my knees up, enveloping them in my arms. "Why are you doing this?"

"This?"

"This." I gestured around the room, referring to the whole cabin and our sudden escape. "Why have you brought me here?"

He smiled softly. "To be honest, I don't know."

I studied him, noticing the tiredness around his eyes and the strain on his handsome face for the first time. "You say you enjoy this life. But do you really? Is it what you want, or what you're doing to please your father?"

He refilled our glasses and lifted his to his lips, looking over the rim at me. "Both, but..." He frowned as he struggled with how to say what he needed to. "But since you I have questioned everything."

"Why since me?" I took a sip of my own wine and settled further back in my chair.

"Because I've destroyed your last days. I've taken so much from you that suddenly it all seems... wrong."

"But surely you knew this was wrong well before me?"

He sighed. "Mae, there are things about me that you don't know, nor need to know. My life hasn't exactly been conventional or easy. I've fought to live as you have. I have struggled with pain and guilt, just as you have. But where we're different is that I deliver and you receive. But suddenly you're delivering the guilt, the questions of what is wrong and right and then... something else. Something deep inside that I don't recognise and if I'm honest, I don't want to recognise."

"You don't recognise emotion?"

He scoffed bitterly. "Oh I recognise emotion, just not this type or this intensely. I don't like it, I hate it. It threatens to take over and drown me."

"And what emotion is it?"

"It doesn't matter." He snapped upright. "You won't be here to understand it, so there is no point in accepting it."

My chest ached as his bitterness slapped me. He sighed and turned back to me. "I'm sorry. I didn't mean to be so heartless."

"It's fine. It's the truth. There's no point to lies at this stage."

We gazed at each other, hurt and devastation ruling the atmosphere between us. Guilt consumed me and I straightened my back. "But there is something you should know."

He quirked an eyebrow and crossed his arms over his chest as he leant back against the worktop. "Go on."

I fidgeted, drawing my knees higher as if they would protect me. "Tony."

His brows lifted and he nodded. "Tony?"

"Yes." My mouth dried but I pushed on. I needed him to know. I wasn't sure why. After everything, I should still hate him but I couldn't bring myself to. I wanted and needed to die with an open heart, without anything weighing me down. "He's... he's..."

"Undercover," he finished for me.

My eyes bulged. "You know?"

He smirked. "I'm not blind, Mae. I knew there was something about him. His bids were excessively high and it's my job to do my homework on our clients. He isn't on any database, nor does he have reliable references. You recognised him immediately and that in itself alerted me to something about him."

"What have you done?"

He rolled his eyes and sighed. "It doesn't concern you now."

"But it does," I argued as I shot out of my chair. "He's getting Lola out. You can't interfere. She doesn't deserve this as much as I didn't, as much as none of your victims did."

"Mae…"

"You can't play with people's lives, Daniel. You need to stop this now. It's not right, it's turning you into a monster and I know you aren't one. You're far from the devil you try to portray yourself as."

"Mae, listen to me…"

"No!" I pushed at him as terror at Lola's future hung in the balance. "You have to get her out!"

"I HAVE!" he shouted to make himself heard over my frantic rambling. "She's safe, lamb. She's safe." A sob erupted as he framed my face with his hands and made me look at him. "Lola is safe. Okay?"

"Are you sure? You're not just saying that to shut me up?"

"God damn it!" He stepped back and pulled a phone from his pocket. "It's me," he said into the phone. "I need you to speak with Mae and tell her Lola is with you. She won't believe me."

I took the phone from him when he pushed it angrily at me. I frowned and hesitantly lifted the phone to my ear. "Hello?"

"Mae?"

"Yes." The voice was familiar but yet I couldn't place it. "Who is this?" He chuckled lightly and my eyes widened. "Frank?"

"Hello, sweetheart." His stutter was completely gone and my jaw dropped. "I know it's a little hard to understand at the moment but you need to trust Daniel now. I have Lola with me and we're both safe." Lola shouted in the background and the sound of her happy voice choked me.

"Okay." It was all I could say as confusion rendered me silent.

"Mae?"

"I'm here."

"Listen. I... I won't have another chance to say this but I... well I just wanted to let you know how much I admire you. You are one strong woman and I know as long as I live that I will never meet another beautiful soul like you. You stuck up for what you know is right no matter the consequences to yourself and I know... I know you will be rewarded for that." I couldn't speak as his kind words twisted at my heart. He knew I was struggling. "May you find your peace, Mae Swift."

I nodded. "And you, Frank. Goodbye."

"Goodbye, sweetheart," he whispered back as his voice tightened. "Goodbye."

Daniel took the phone from me and took me into his body tightly. The situation hit me suddenly and I sobbed into him. "I'm going to die," I whispered against him. "I..."

"Sshhh." He held me closer, pulling me tight as I let it go.

"I'm so scared. I... I'm frightened of what..."

"I know, Mae. I've sorted it, don't worry."

I reared back and looked up at him. "You've sorted what? How can you even *sort* this?"

He looked apprehensive and I frowned at him. "When I asked you if you wanted the choice of when you would go. You told me yes." I nodded but I still didn't understand. "Well, now you get to choose, lamb. You get to pick the time you go. Not God, not the pain, not even your own body, but you. I brought something with me that... that will lead you peacefully to where you need to go."

I stared at him, swallowing back the unknown. "You... we do this together?"

He nodded, his eyes widening as dampness glistened in his eyes. "Yes. We do it together. You won't ever be alone again. I promise."

I nodded firmly as my throat closed in. He stepped towards me and took my hand, watching the way I curled my fingers around his. "It's the least I can do now. I owe you peace, Mae. I owe you your final moments and I promise to make them as... tender as possible. Do you understand what I'm saying?"

I nodded. "But I still need to hear it, Daniel."

He shook his head. "The words will never come. I'm incapable of feeling, Mae but I need you to know that yes, with you I finally feel my heart beating faster and harder. I feel the need to give pleasure without taking. I feel it inside me, the warmth, the pain, the guilt, and for that alone I know how hard this will be but still I will make sure you leave me with a smile on your beautiful face."

He brought his mouth to mine and showed me without words how he felt. The tenderness and gentility in his kiss wound around my soul and soothed it. His tongue slowly traced the edge of mine as he slipped his fingers through my hair and held me as tight as he possibly could. His lips moulded to mine as he drove adoration into me, expressing how he felt without a declaration.

I closed my eyes and ran my nose down his when he rested his forehead against mine. "Then I will say it," I whispered. "I love you."

His grip on my hair tightened as a funny sound echoed in his chest. He was almost desperate as he pushed me back against the wall and continued to kiss me. His passion and need governed him this time and the kiss was hungry and demanding.

He placed his hands under my bottom and lifted me, urging me to wrap my legs around his waist. He didn't waste time as he scrambled with the hem of my dress and yanked it up around my waist before he thrust deep inside me. My head dropped back and we both groaned in pleasure as I shifted my hips to accommodate him easier.

"Oh God," he breathed as he rested his head in the crook of my shoulder. "You are so damn perfect." His thrusts quickened as he slammed deeper and deeper into me. "You were made for me, lamb. This is so wrong." The strain in his voice hurt my soul and devastation clenched at my heart.

"Then make it right before I go, Daniel."

He looked at me, his eyes full of sorrow. "It's too late for me."

"No," I whispered as I stroked his hair from his forehead and pulled him to me. "It's never too late. Your heart is bigger than you think. Let it take you where you need to go. Fall in love, Daniel. Find someone who loves you so much that it's painful. Let her hold your hand, and let her guide you."

Tears streamed down my face as I begged him to take what he could from life and live it. "I need you to

carry on when I'm gone. Find her, Daniel. Find her."
He stared at me in shock. "Her name is Annabelle
Rose. I placed her in foster care. You need to find her
and give her a family. Promise me."

He nodded feverishly. "I promise, Mae. I will find
her and I will keep her safe. I will nurture her and
love her. I will tell her how God damned fucking
special her mother was. I'll tell her how much love
you had for her and how you perfected motherhood
by being selfless and giving her a chance at life."

He drove into me and I cried out as my heart broke
and my orgasm liberated my sobs. He clung to me, his
own distress heavy as he took my sobs and soaked
them up.

"Tomorrow," I whispered.

He nodded; he knew what I meant. His eyes held
mine as we both braved the burden tomorrow would
bring. But I was ready, finally ready. I was tired of
living and I needed the journey into oblivion to stop
the hatred and pain inside me.

"Tomorrow, Mae Swift."

"What's your surname?" I asked. I suddenly
wanted to know, I had no idea why.

He chuckled and smirked. "Why, lamb, I am
Shepherd. I've told you once." He tapped my nose
playfully. "My name is Daniel Shepherd."

Chapter Twenty Two

'And so it ends.'

"Good morning." He grinned at me. I could see the pain behind his smile but I smiled back, refusing to let the weight of the day spoil my final moments. "Any pain?"

"No." I smiled widely hoping the tumour would permit me my final moments pain free. "All's good at the mo."

He nodded and perched beside me on the bed. He motioned for me to sit up and I did, allowing him to rest the tray on my lap. Amazing scents of croissant, jam and coffee fired up my senses and my mouth watered. "Wow, this is perfect. Thank you."

I picked up the cup of coffee and took a sip, watching Daniel over the rim. "Everything okay?"

"Sure." He nodded and took a deep breath. "Hunky-dory, darling."

The coffee burnt my throat on the way down when I heard the emotion in his voice constricting the passage, making the hot liquid struggle to find a route through. "Daniel." He looked at me, the pain in his expression even deeper. "If... if you can't do this then that's fine, you know. I'll just wait until..."

He shook his head. "No. It's fine."

He didn't speak again as he stood from the bed and disappeared into the little en-suite that joined the room. I studied his muscular back, each perfect muscle rippling on his journey across the room. His shoulders were bunched, stress and tension pulling at his beautiful body.

The coffee suddenly tasted a little bitter. I placed it back on the tray and picked up the croissant, pulling off small pieces and popping them in my mouth. My gaze wandered out of the small window and I smiled as the sun welcomed me. Everything seemed to be brighter, crisper. Either that or I was more aware. The sky rippled as though dancing in the rays of the hot sun.

"No," I whispered when panic set in. "Not today, please. Not today." I squeezed my eyes closed and prayed. Prayed for my sanity to be complete when all I had left was hours. I wouldn't allow the tumour to twist and morph my final moments. It wasn't fair.

"Hey." Daniel's voice broke my concentration. I opened my eyes to him. He was stood with a towel around his hips, water dripping from his hair and down his delicious body. He couldn't have showered that quickly. He'd only been in the room a matter of seconds. "Are you okay?"

I nodded and forced a smile, knowing I'd lost precious moments of time. "Yeah."

He eyed me warily, suspicious of my false smile. He knew. I could read it in his eyes. "Is it getting worse?" His voice was tight, uncontrolled as pain closed his eyes.

"I'm fine," I said as I took a deep breath and climbed from the bed.

Tears unexpectedly formed and I covered my mouth with my hand to try and contain the sob that wanted to be free. My chest stuttered and I stared at him in a panic. "Hey," he whispered as he hurried over to me. "It's okay. It's okay."

I nodded briskly and literally dived for him, needing him to just hold me and make everything alright. "I'm so scared."

"I know, lamb. But I'm here and I'll be here right through to the end. I promise I won't let you feel pain. I promise."

I nodded and let him hold me. Life suddenly seemed so cruel. It had taken everything from me and when I had finally touched something good, something right, it viciously took it away again.

I blew out a breath, telling myself to be strong as I looked up at him. "I'm so sorry."

He frowned and cocked his head. "What for?"

"For doing this to you. This is not something you'll ever... forget and yet you're willing to do it for me."

He scoffed bitterly and shook his head. "Oh, lamb." He brushed a thumb over my tears and rolled his lips. "Why the hell didn't I just leave you? Tell Franco I couldn't find you?"

"We do what we have to, Daniel." He stared at me and I could practically taste his guilt. "I don't hold grudges. I forgive you."

"But how? How can you do that?"

I shrugged. "It's just how I am. What's the point in regrets? It never changes things, it just makes them worse. Life is dealt like a pack of cards. What your hand holds is what you have to play with. It's how it is and I refuse to cheat. I won't steal someone else's hand, nor will I take what I am not given. So I accept it, accept my fate like the five cards dealt. It's just my time to fold now."

He smiled sadly and brushed a kiss over my forehead. "And I can promise this game will stay with me for the rest of my life, Mae. Those five cards are the ones that will stay up my sleeve forever. I won't ever forget. And I won't let our daughter forget."

He tilted my face towards him and kissed me softly, every emotion running through his veins was directed into me.

We both blew out a breath and nodded. "Come on." He tapped my backside and smiled. "We're off out for a while."

"Oh, okay." I smiled, grateful for the change in direction.

I swallowed back the ache in my chest and the need to tell him I loved him once more. He knew and it wouldn't help anything to repeat things. I knew he cared for me, and after years of loneliness, the way he looked at me and touched me told me everything I needed to know.

I laughed loudly as he ran after me, the kite thrashing in the air behind me and the string wrapping itself around my wrist. "My God, you can run fast!" he exclaimed when he finally caught up with me, whipping me up into his arms and swinging me round. The kite twirled in the air as Daniel tackled me onto the sand.

I laughed even louder when he buried his face in my breasts and growled loudly. "It's these long legs."

Daniel scoffed and slid a hand up the length of my legs until his fingers tickled the hem on my shorts. "Lamb, come on. Even millipedes have longer legs than you."

I slapped him playfully and pouted. "I'll have you know these legs won the eight hundred metre race at school... In record time I might add."

He grinned at me, mischief twinkling in his eyes. "I bet you were a right little terror in school."

I placed a hand on my chest and gaped at him. "Who? Me? Never!"

"Mm-hmm." He twirled his tongue up the side of my neck and started to nibble on my ear lobe generating a shiver and an inner throb.

"What were you like? I bet you were a right randy hormonal teenager."

He laughed and nipped the skin on my neck with the edge of his teeth. "You know me so well."

I giggled and slapped him. "I'm hungry."

"Mmm, me too." He rested his hands beside my head and looked at me with a warm smile. "And what does her ladyship fancy?"

"Apart from you?" I wiggled my eyebrows and smirked. "We're at the seaside, Daniel."

He smiled and nodded as he pulled me up from the sand. "Fish and chips it is."

We passed a young boy digging in the sand beside his parents. I gestured to them with the kite and they smiled and nodded allowing me to hand it to the little boy. "Don't get it caught in the clouds," I whispered to him.

He grinned and giggled before he pulled his dad off his deckchair and dragged him onto an open part of the beach.

Daniel looked at me with a curious expression. "Come to think of it, you were quite the expert with the kite."

"Yeah, my dad taught me." Pain crippled my heart when I thought of my father and how the discovery of his lies had ruined my happy memories.

Daniel slipped his arm around me and pulled me close. "Whatever your father did or didn't do, he's still your father and he loved you very much."

"Did you know him?" I asked.

"No, not really. I'd seen him around the house a couple of times but I was only young so I didn't take much notice."

"I thought he was a good man."

Daniel sighed. "We all think that of our parents, lamb. And I suppose in their own way, they are. They still love us, no matter what they do in life. We have a daughter, we haven't participated in her life whatsoever but yet we still love her."

I gazed at him and smiled. "Yes."

He returned my smile then turned to the kiosk we came across and ordered our food. We found a bench on the pier and ate in silence as we watched children run and play on the sand, their laughter loud in the air around us. The little boy with the kite had the loudest, happiest chuckle I had ever heard and the way his dad swung him and tickled him gave me such a happy feeling.

"Promise you'll bring Annabelle here."

Daniel looked at me. His eyes filled with tears but as soon as they appeared, they vanished. "I promise," he said with a small smile.

I blinked when a blue butterfly fluttered its wings around my head. The small flap of its wings in front of my face made me gasp. It hovered around me, its beautiful elegance reminding me that it was nearly time.

"Holly Blue," Daniel whispered as we watched it quiver in the breeze.

It shimmered, its tiny hairs rippling as it appeared to stare at me. "It's time to go."

Daniel didn't argue. He took my food from me, placed it in a nearby bin, and held out his hand to me. He curled his fingers around mine and I shivered when something tickled my arm. We both gazed in awe as the butterfly brushed over our hands then flew away.

It was time.

I stared in silence at the mass of fairy lights decorating the room when we stepped inside the cottage. Each tiny white light lit a section of the room, making it appear serene and romantic. Numerous large candles dotted the space, their flickering creating rhythmic movement over the cream walls, making the paintwork appear to dance. Flowers of every single description and scent covered the furniture. My eyes fell on the ginormous fluffy rug in front of the open log fire. Flames high and low jumped almost angrily in the fireplace, heating the chill in the room.

"Oh my..."

I struggled for breath, emotion clogging my pores and my throat.

"You need to go change," Daniel whispered in my ear. "You'll find everything you need in the bedroom."

I nodded. I couldn't speak. He brought my knuckles to his lips and kissed me gently. His soft smile echoed his thoughts, his eyes sad but full of some other emotion.

"It will be okay, Daniel. I'm ready now."

He sank his teeth into his lip and winced but determination took over and he nodded. "Go."

I nodded and climbed the stairs.

My legs finally gave way when I saw the dress that hung from a hanger in the bedroom. A sob curled its way up my throat and my body shook with both heartache and happiness.

The soft cream lace of the dress shimmered in the lamplight, the tiny diamante butterflies nestled into the fabric reaching for me as if delighted they were with me.

I stood and walked over to it, my hand on my mouth as I tried to quieten my weeping. How Daniel even knew about my love of this dress, never mind purchasing it and bringing it here was too much to take. "Oh, dear God," I whispered as I blew out a breath and tried to control myself. My eyes then landed on the bed where exquisite cream underwear sat waiting for me to slide into. Cream heels perched on the floor beside the bed.

I ran a finger over the material and smiled. I wasn't sure my heart could accommodate anymore love for a man that had taken so much from me, but right then, I thought death would come too quickly as it beat frantically and violently.

I pulled off my shorts and t-shirt and walked into the shower.

My breath stunted when I stepped off the last step and saw Daniel waiting for me. He was wearing the suit that had been on display with the dress in the shop window. The material covered his fine body as though it had been specifically made for him and I'm not too proud to say I drooled. Soft music played in the background, the sultry sounds of a slow track serenely comforting.

He stared at me, his eyes running up and down my body. "My God," he muttered. "You are... wow."

I smiled and looked down at myself. "Thank you... for this. How did you know?"

He smiled. "Remember, I watched you. Every day you passed that window you would stop and stare."

He smiled sheepishly and I stepped towards him and took his hand in mine.

"Well, thank you. You have no idea how much this means."

He slid his hand into his inside jacket pocket and pulled out a long, thin velvet box. I stared at it. I knew what it was before I even opened it. "Daniel…"

"Sshhh." He shook his head and opened the box. The blue diamond that sat on the end of the platinum chain took my breath. Daniel didn't wait; he slipped it from the box and gestured for me to turn around. I did as he asked, my body tingling in awareness when he lifted my long hair and encouraged me to hold it out of his way. He positioned the diamond around my neck and fastened the clasp, then placed a soft kiss on the nape of my neck. "You look beautiful."

He shook himself off and tugged me over to a small round table at the edge of the room. He lifted silver domes from the plates before he pulled out a chair for me. I smiled happily and sat, allowing him to tuck me in before he poured glasses of wine for both of us.

The dinner looked amazing, different colours of gorgeous but light foods that held delicate and tempting aromas.

Daniel held up his glass and I lifted mine too. "To new friendships and," he paused, his eyes locked on mine, "and to doing what's right."

I echoed him and took a sip. "What will you do now?" I asked when we started to eat.

"What is right."

"And that is?" I probed as I chewed on the most exquisite honeyed prawn I had ever tasted.

"Find my daughter. Put the past where it belongs and teach her what is right."

"Thank you," I whispered to him. He nodded. "You'll find all you need to find her in my apartment. There's a box in the bottom of my wardrobe, all the paperwork is in there."

"Anything else you need me to do?"

"No, not really. Just take care of Annabelle."

We ate in silence, both of us struggling to swallow with what was before us. It was becoming harder to stop thinking about what was to come. He flicked his gaze to me frequently, as I did him.

"Oh," I suddenly said. "What is it with Frank? How come he lost his stutter?"

He smiled guiltily. "It's all part of the game. He gains your trust and relates back to me the things you confide in him." I tutted and rolled my eyes. "But he genuinely likes you, Mae. He was rather angry with me over you. He told me how you stuck up for him when Demi was her usual self towards him."

"And the whore?"

"The whore?" he questioned with high eyebrows.

"Demi."

"Ahh. Yes, Demi is somewhat... Demi."

"Mmm," I mumbled.

He smirked, his eyes glistening in the candlelight. "Are you jealous, lamb?"

I laughed. "Yes, I'm not too proud to tell you that. But, Daniel." He nodded, urging me to continue. "I don't want her near Annabelle."

He smiled arrogantly. "You needn't worry about that."

"Oh?"

He peered at his watch. "Well round about now, my father and his minions are in the company of Tony."

My eyes widened. "What?"

He regarded me as he bit a green bean off his fork. "For the sake of Annabelle, I did a deal with Tony. Because of your connection with him, I gave him details of everything if he allowed me to bring up my daughter. Of course with an opportunity like that, he granted me grace."

My heart swelled with pride. "You have no idea how happy that makes me. I need to know that Annabelle will be okay before I go and you just granted me that."

He shrugged. "You taught me many things, Mae. One of which is that it's okay to take the hard way. That the struggle makes it all the more worth it. Raising Annabelle will be the toughest thing I ever have to do but you have shown me that love is far superior to hatred, and I want that. I want to wake in the morning and not feel this damn bitterness that consumes me. I want to look at the morning sun and feel its warmth instead of noticing the bite of ice on the grass, or the single cloud that darkens the sky. I need to look for the good things, and I need to show them to Annabelle instead of allowing her to focus on that grey cloud. I want to share happy times with her and I want us to be there for one another after you're gone."

"You have given me so much, Daniel."

He frowned at me, confused by my sudden words.

"You gave me the ability to feel. After… well after the first time I met you, life was such a struggle. Especially when I found out I was pregnant. And then when I had her, handing her over was ultimately the hardest thing I've ever faced." I gestured to the slice on my face. "I swore that no man would ever come near me again. That way I couldn't be broken anymore. So I cut my face and made myself repulsive."

Daniel sighed but shook his head. "But you see, Mae, I never see it. I see you, what's buried deep inside you. The goodness and the strength that leaves me in awe with every damn breath I take."

"And you gave me something else." I carried on. "You gave me the ability to love and…" I watched as his eyes watered. "…And feel loved."

He swallowed but didn't give me what I wanted to hear. Instead he stood and walked around the table to me. He slid his arms around me and lifted me from the chair and carried me over to the rug in front of the fire. He stood me up, dropping my feet carefully to the ground.

He circled me, his hand sliding over the soft fabric of my dress on his route. "I've been desperate to peel you out of this as soon as I saw you in it."

I blew out a breath and closed my eyes when he slid the zip down that had taken me ages to do up. He pushed the fabric over my shoulders and I watched it sink to the floor around my ankles.

"Much better," he mumbled behind me as he ran a finger down the length of my spine. Birdy's *Skinny Love* started to play as Daniel unhooked my bra. His hands moved around me until he was cupping my breasts gently. "You have beautiful breasts, lamb. The most exquisite soft flesh and perfect pink nipples."

I moaned faintly when he ran the tip of his finger around a nipple, making it swell instantly and pucker for him. He splayed a hand on my stomach as he moved his mouth down every ridge of my backbone, his tongue wetting my skin on his journey until he came to a kneeling position behind me.

He dragged my knickers down my legs and urged me to step out of them when they reached my ankles. He chuckled when he flung them onto the fire and they spat angrily. "I always knew your underwear was hot, lamb."

"Well they are now." I laughed. I didn't laugh for long when he slid his finger between my thighs and ran it over my sex, tormenting my clit teasingly as he lightly brushed over it. I circled my hips, trying to get the stimulation I needed. I groaned in frustration when he slid his tongue between my buttocks, probing at my anus as he slipped a finger deep into my pussy. "Always so wet for me, lamb."

My body was strung so tightly it was almost painful. Arousal caused my head to throb and I urged it away, denying it, refusing to let it take this moment away from me.

"Okay?" Daniel asked when he felt me tense.

"Uh-huh," I lied when another fire of pain struck my forehead. I blew out a breath and concentrated on the pleasure riding me higher instead of the agony.

Daniel turned me around so I was facing him. He looked up at me from where he knelt. "When did you undress?" I asked when I stared at his long cock stood proudly against his stomach. The head glistened with pre-cum, tempting me.

His eyes widened when I fell to my knees before him and immediately wrapped my hand around his shaft. "Shit," he hissed when I bent forward and took him into my mouth. His hand fisted my hair as my tongue devoured the moisture that was just for me. His taste made my taste buds tingle, making me greedy for more. He groaned loudly as I started stroking the underside of his cock with each bob of my head. "Jesus Christ, darling."

I smiled around his length and licked the tiny slit with the tip of my tongue. He growled and lifted me, positioning me until I was knelt over his lap, my thighs on either side of his. He lowered me down onto him slowly. My back arched as pleasure forced my body to shiver in bliss. "Oh God," he breathed as his chest stuttered. He closed his eyes as he allowed the ecstasy to take him.

Queen's, *Who Wants To Live Forever* played in the background as we made love. The words took me along as I moved slowly on my lover. His eyes held mine as his hands held my shoulders and he kissed every single inch of skin on my chest, his lips pulling at my nipples occasionally as he let me take control. Sweat trickled from both of us as the flames from the fire heated our skin. I refused to move faster, taking him slowly but deeply. He allowed it, his face showing rapture the whole way through, a mirror image of my own.

My orgasm started in my toes and pulled every single muscle in my body on its way up to my brain. "I love you," I cried out as paradise took me to heaven before my body did.

He roared and buried his face in my chest as he came violently inside me, his body jerking as he clung to me. I held him to me, inhaling his scent, consuming his touch, feeding from his emotion. I squeezed my eyes closed as another wave of pain caused my body to tense.

"Are you ready?"

His words were full of pain and despair. He swallowed and I watched the bob of his throat. "Yes."

He knew it was coming, the pain. He sensed my need to leave pain free. He nodded slowly and bit his lip. He pulled me off his lap and lay me down in front of the fire. Time seemed to stop as he reached for a small box by the side of the fire. His eyes locked with mine, silently questioning but I nodded. "I'm ready."

He closed his eyes and blew out an uneven breath then took the syringe from the box. He stared at it for a long time. "Daniel."

He nodded and gulped before he ran his finger over a spot of skin on my arm. "How long will it take?" I asked when he inserted it into my arm and pressed the plunger.

"I... I don't know."

He was struggling to talk and I watched as his chest stuttered wildly. He placed the empty syringe on the table and manoeuvred his body until he was laid beside me.

The Moody Blues *Nights In White Satin* began to softly fill the air as we gazed at each other. Warmth trickled over me, a calmness that seemed to liquefy inside me. The music flowed peacefully as the depth to Daniel's eyes held me and comforted me in my last moments.

"Promise me you'll fall in love, Daniel."

He nodded. He couldn't speak as he watched life drain from me. Pain morphed into tranquillity, anguish calmed, bringing with it a sense of acceptance. The edges blurred as my heart slowed. My eyes closed as Daniel grabbed at my hand. "Mae…" he whispered. The Moody Blues sang out that they loved me as my Mother appeared, a tiny blue butterfly flickering in the light beside her. My breath caught as she stood smiling at me. She reached out for me and I slipped my hand into hers, the sweet gentleness of her wrapping me up and holding me tight to make the next journey.

"Mae…" I heard his urgent voice echo somewhere in my head as I stepped towards my mother.

"Mmm," I murmured. It was all I could manage in my last moments.

"Mae… God damn it," he cried as I felt his hands caress my face. "I love you. I love you, Mae Swift."

I died with a smile. I died with the taste of Daniel's tears on my lips. I died with a full heart. And I died with no regrets.

Life had given me what it needed to. It had eventually given me what I had craved. The love of a man I knew deep down inside was good and worthy of loving my daughter.

Life was cruel. But yet I had accepted its punishing taunts and that in itself had allowed me to gain the most treasured possession it could grant.

Peace.

Love.

Epilogue

'And so it begins.'

Daniel

Two years later

I smiled when her soft voice tickled my ears. She scurried around and I squeezed my fingers around hers when she slipped her tiny hand into mine. "I think Mummy needs more of those yellow flowers, Daddy."

I nodded and smiled at her. "The daffodils?"

She nodded firmly. "Yes, those ones."

Her little voice cheerily sang the words to *Somewhere over the Rainbow* as her head bobbed happily and she weeded her Mother's graveside.

"You sing like an angel, Annie."

"Mummy would like my singing."

"Mummy would love your singing. She would be very proud of you."

She smiled up at me, her rosy cheeks bright with pride. "I think Mummy would be proud of you too, Daddy, cos' you're the best daddy in the world."

Her little arms enveloped me and I lifted her up, her short chubby legs wrapping around my waist as she slid her arms around my neck and planted a wet kiss on my cheek.

She gasped loudly and giggled. "Look, Daddy, Holly's back."

I moved my gaze to Mae's gravestone and smiled softly at the tiny blue butterfly that visited us regularly. "Good morning, lamb."

It fluttered its wings and scurried across the top of the stone. "Why do you always call it, lamb, Daddy? Its name is Holly."

I smiled softly, remembering. "It's just Daddy being silly, honey."

"Is it because our name is Shepherd and that butterfly is your lamb?"

Her tiny blue eyes regarded me. My heart swelled with so much love that it caused me to gasp. "A shepherd always cares for its lambs, Annie. It looks after them, nurtures them and hopes that they will flourish under the care and devotion he gives them. And he knows one day, when they have learnt to accept that love, that they will gain what they most crave."

"And what do lambs crave?"

I smiled as I stroked a finger over the headstone and walked towards the car. "Just love, Annie. That's all she ever wanted. Just love."

The end

Turn the page for a sneak peak of

THE SALVATION OF DANIEL

Book 2 in the Blue Butterfly Series

THE SALVATION OF DANIEL
By D H Sidebottom

Mae had taught me many things; the ability to smile, that hope was a real ideal and most of all that I was worthy of love. Annie also showed me that. She showed me how to see the good things in life. How to sing with the birds every morning, how to laugh when flour and egg decorated the kitchen walls and how to feel the warmth of the sun every day.

She also proved that I could love with an engulfing force. And I did. I loved my daughter with every fibre of me and every raw nerve that had once only felt pain. My heart swelled with each of her cheeky smiles and every single sweet echo of her voice.

My daughter was very much her mother's child. From the lustre of her ebony hair to her twinkling sky blue eyes and from the way her smile lifted my heart, to the way her stubborn side exasperated me.

I was strong in my beliefs. Determined to raise her the way her mother had wanted me to. But Annie, like Mae, found the funny side to life so effortlessly. She laughed easily and frequently, she delighted in simple things and braved each daily troubles optimistically.

And I followed her. She taught me how to live as I taught her how to grow.

And just as I relaxed into life as a father, my father found his way back into mine.
As did Connie, Mae's dead sister.

COMING WINTER 2014

Printed in Great Britain
by Amazon